Writing the Critical Essay

Assisted Suicide

An OPPOSING VIEWPOINTS® Guide

Other books in the Writing the Critical Essay series are:

Abortion
Alcohol
Animal Rights
Cloning
The Death Penalty
Eating Disorders
Energy Alternatives
Global Warming
Illegal Immigration
Marijuana
The Patriot Act
Prisons
Racism
School Violence
Smoking
Terrorism

Writing the Critical Essay

Assisted
Suicide

An OPPOSING ◼ VIEWPOINTS® Guide

Lauri S. Friedman, *Book Editor*

Christine Nasso, *Publisher*
Elizabeth Des Chenes, *Managing Editor*

OPPOSING
VIEWPOINTS®
SERIES

GREENHAVEN PRESS
An imprint of Thomson Gale, a part of The Thomson Corporation

THOMSON
━━━✦━━━
GALE

Detroit • New York • San Francisco • New Haven, Conn. • Waterville, Maine • London

LIBRARY OF CONGRESS CATALOGING-IN-PUBLICATION DATA
Assisted suicide / Lauri S. Friedman, book editor.
p. cm. — (Writing the critical essay)
Includes bibliographical references and index.
ISBN-13: 978-0-7377-3640-3 (hardcover : alk. paper)
ISBN-10: 0-7377-3640-2 (hardcover : alk. paper)
1. Assisted suicide—Juvenile literature. I. Friedman, Lauri S.
R726.A853 2007
179.7—dc22
2006027183

CONTENTS

Examining the state of writing and how it is taught in the United States was the official purpose of the National Commission on Writing in America's Schools and Colleges. The commission, made up of teachers, school administrators, business leaders, and college and university presidents, released its first report in 2003. "Despite the best efforts of many educators," commissioners argued, "writing has not received the full attention it deserves." Among the findings of the commission was that most fourth-grade students spent less than three hours a week writing, that three-quarters of high school seniors never receive a writing assignment in their history or social studies classes, and that more than 50 percent of first-year students in college have problems writing error-free papers. The commission called for a "cultural sea change" that would increase the emphasis on writing for both elementary and secondary schools. These conclusions have made some educators realize that writing must be emphasized in the curriculum. As colleges are demanding an ever-higher level of writing proficiency from incoming students, schools must respond by making students more competent writers. In response to these concerns, the SAT, an influential standardized test used for college admissions, required an essay for the first time in 2005.

Books in the Writing the Critical Essay: An Opposing Viewpoints Guide series use the patented Opposing Viewpoints format to help students learn to organize ideas and arguments and to write essays using common critical writing techniques. Each book in the series focuses on a particular type of essay writing—including expository, persuasive, descriptive, and narrative—that students learn while being taught both the five-paragraph essay as well as longer pieces of writing that have an opinionated focus. These guides include everything necessary to help students research, outline, draft, edit, and ultimately write successful essays across the curriculum, including essays for the SAT.

Using Opposing Viewpoints

This series is inspired by and builds upon Greenhaven Press's acclaimed Opposing Viewpoints series. As in the parent series, each book in the Writing the Critical Essay series focuses on a timely and controversial social issue that provides lots of opportunities for creating thought-provoking essays. The first section of each volume begins with a brief introductory essay that provides context for the opposing viewpoints that follow. These articles are chosen for their accessibility and clearly stated views. The thesis of each article is made explicit in the article's title and is accentuated by its pairing with an opposing or alternative view. These essays are both models of persuasive writing techniques and valuable research material that students can mine to write their own informed essays. Guided reading and discussion questions help lead students to key ideas and writing techniques presented in the selections.

The second section of each book begins with a preface discussing the format of the essays and examining characteristics of the featured essay type. Model five-paragraph and longer essays then demonstrate that essay type. The essays are annotated so that key writing elements and techniques are pointed out to the student. Sequential, step-by-step exercises help students construct and refine thesis statements; organize material into outlines; analyze and try out writing techniques; write transitions, introductions, and conclusions; and incorporate quotations and other researched material. Ultimately, students construct their own compositions using the designated essay type.

The third section of each volume provides additional research material and writing prompts to help the student. Additional facts about the topic of the book serve as a convenient source of supporting material for essays. Other features help students go beyond the book for their research. Like other Greenhaven Press books, each book in the Writing the Critical Essay series includes bibliographic listings of relevant periodical articles, books, Web sites, and organizations to contact.

Writing the Critical Essay: An Opposing Viewpoints Guide will help students master essay techniques that can be used in any discipline.

Background to Controversy: Oregon's Death with Dignity Act

I n 1997 the citizens of Oregon voted to legalize a highly controversial practice called physician-assisted suicide in their state. They passed what is called the Death with Dignity Act, which allows a terminally ill person meeting certain criteria to end his or her own life with the help of a doctor. In typical cases, a physician can comply with a dying patient's request for a prescription for a lethal dosage of medication. The patient then voluntarily takes the medication at his or her discretion, usually at home surrounded by family members. Though this practice is controversial, few people actually take advantage of physician-assisted suicide. Only about one in every eight hundred deaths in the state is attributed to physician-assisted suicide. According to the 2006 Eighth Annual Report on the Death with Dignity Act, 17 percent of dying patients in Oregon discussed the option with their families but only about 2 percent ended up requesting prescriptions from physicians. But even though the practice is minimally used, it continues to fuel debates in Oregon and other states, including Washington, California, Michigan, and Maine, where citizens have made attempts to pass similar legislation. Indeed, Oregon's groundbreaking Death with Dignity Act has people all over the country discussing whether the practice is safe, ethical, and fair, and whether it should be available to all Americans.

Safeguards Against Abuse?

The Death with Dignity Act was written with several safeguards that are intended to protect the vulnerable, weak, sick, elderly, and others from being taken advantage of. To

A suicide machine's canister holds the lethal medicines that the user will inject.

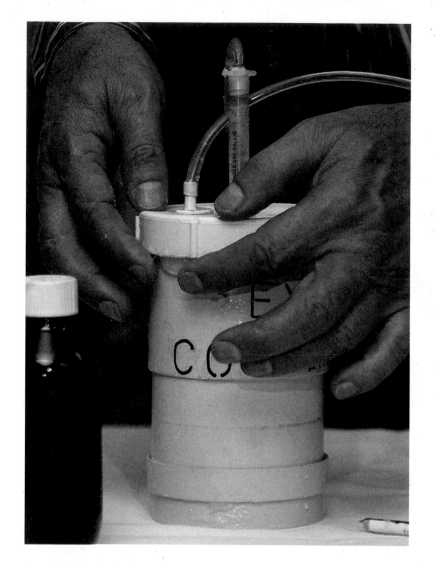

be eligible for physician-assisted suicide under the act, a patient must be eighteen years or older, an Oregon resident, able to make and communicate one's own health care decisions, and diagnosed with a terminal illness with a prognosis of six months or less to live. This last precaution is meant to protect both doctors and patients from acting hastily or giving in to suicidal impulses when death is not imminent. The law further requires that the patient make two verbal requests for assistance—separated by fifteen days—to a doctor, have these requests witnessed by two individuals who are not caregivers or family members, and be able to rescind the request for the lethal medication at any time. Furthermore, patients must be able to self-administer the prescription; this limits the doctor's role to assisting in the act versus directly taking a life. Finally, the patient's terminal diagnosis must be certified by a second physician, who must confirm that the patient is mentally competent to make health care decisions. All of these precautions are meant to prevent doctors or family members from profiting from a person's death or from unduly influencing someone to end his or her life.

Some patients wish to undergo assisted suicide to end the physical and emotional pain of an illness.

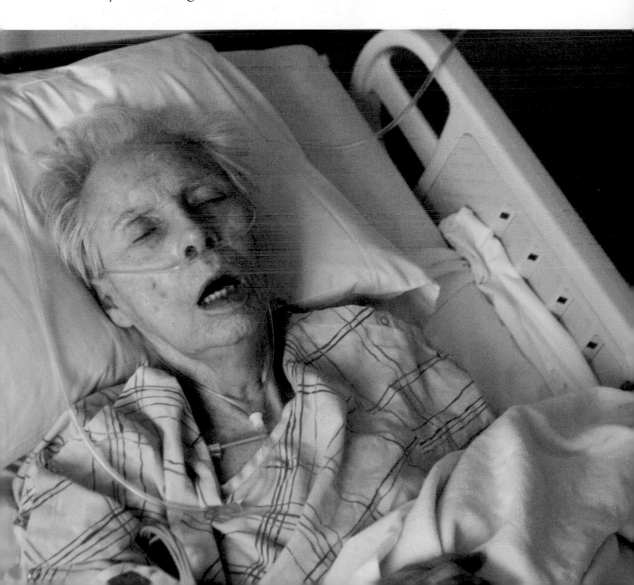

Opponents of assisted suicide, however, are not convinced such safeguards provide adequate protection. Nor do they believe that assisted suicide should be promoted as an option for a dying person, arguing that the medical profession should devote its efforts toward making dying people more comfortable and relieving pain. Such advocates call for improvements to what is called end-of-life or palliative (symptom-relieving) care. Besides pain-relief medication, palliative care includes respiratory machines, feeding tubes, and other devices used with the aim of relieving symptoms, not curing the underlying illness. Failing to opt for palliative care, according to the group Physicians for Compassionate Care, sends the message that "doctors

Demonstrators, some of whom are disabled, protest physician-assisted suicide in Washington DC in 2005.

can do a better job of killing patients than they can of caring for their medical needs," and consider assisted suicide to be "the ultimate abandonment of a patient by a doctor."[1] For these reasons, opponents of assisted suicide view the Death with Dignity Act as wrongly promoting death over life. Debra J. Saunders, who has spearheaded an effort to reject a Death-with-Dignity-style law in California, says, "There is true rot in a state that regards those who want to kill the sick as more compassionate than those who want to treat the sick."[2]

At a news conference, cancer patients react to the Supreme Court ruling upholding Oregon's physician-assisted suicide law.

"Peace of Mind" in Oregon

Yet those who have opted for physician-assisted suicide in Oregon appear to have done so wholeheartedly and without coercion. The majority of Oregonians who ended their lives according to the provisions of the Death with Dignity Act in 2006 reportedly did so because they were afraid of being unable to engage in activities that made life enjoyable, and to preserve their dignity and their autonomy. According to the 2006 report on the act, the majority elected the procedure in a clear state of mind and all were subject to the safeguards laid down in the act. Some advocates, such as author Betty Rollin, have described the virtue of the act as follows: "[Physician-assisted suicide] is worth it for a simple reason: peace of mind. . . . That means those who happen to live in the state of Oregon—sick or not— have a kind of insurance the rest of us don't have: They know they can get out of life when they are desperate to do so."[3]

Though the Death with Dignity Act is legal, it is by no means uncontested. It was most recently challenged by the Bush administration, which charged that states do not have the right to allow doctors to prescribe federally controlled substances. On January 17, 2006, however, the Supreme Court ruled 6-3 in favor of Oregon, upholding the law. Though the law is safe for now, there are sure to be more challenges to it, and also to assisted suicide bids in other states. *Writing the Critical Essay: Assisted Suicide* explores some of the key arguments made for and against assisted suicide. It also helps students formulate their own thoughts about the topic. Through skill-building exercises and thoughtful discussion questions, students will articulate their own thoughts about assisted suicide and develop tools to craft their own essays on the subject.

Notes

1. Physicians for Compassionate Care Educational Foundation, "Why Physician-Assisted Suicide Is Wrong and Dangerous," February 25, 2004.

2. Debra J. Saunders, "Death with Vanity," *San Francisco Chronicle*, January 4, 2005.

3. Betty Rollin, "Path to a Peaceful Death," *Washington Post*, May 30, 2004, p. B07.

Section One: Opposing Viewpoints on Assisted Suicide

Assisted Suicide Should Be Legal ~ Good

Peter Singer

In the following viewpoint author Peter Singer argues that physician-assisted suicide should be legal. He claims it is every person's right to make judgments about the quality of his or her own life, which includes deciding how and when it should end. He points to evidence from Oregon and the Netherlands, two places where physician-assisted suicide is legal, to show that the laws have not been abused or used to violate the rights of the vulnerable. Singer concludes that because legal physician-assisted suicide has been shown to be safe and effective, it should be a right granted to all people.

Peter Singer is a professor at Princeton University and a well-known animal rights activist. He has also written extensively on ethical matters concerning poverty, genetic engineering, globalization, and euthanasia.

Consider the following questions:

1. When, according to the author, did Oregon and the Netherlands legalize physician-assisted suicide?
2. According to Singer, about how many Oregonians opt for physician-assisted suicide each year?
3. How does Singer respond to concerns that physician-assisted suicide would be pushed upon the poor, uneducated, and uninsured?

The nineteenth-century philosopher John Stuart Mill argued that individuals are, ultimately, the best judges and guardians of their own interests. So in a famous exam-

Peter Singer, "Making Our Own Decisions About Death," *Free Inquiry*, August/September, 2005, Copyright 2005 Council for Democratic and Secular Humanism, Inc. Reproduced by permission of the author.

ple, he said that if you see people about to cross a bridge you know to be unsafe, you may forcibly stop them in order to inform them of the risk that the bridge may collapse under them, but, if they decide to continue, you must stand aside and let them cross, for only they know the importance to them of crossing and only they know how to balance that against the possible loss of their lives. Mill's example presupposes, of course, that we are dealing with beings who are capable of taking in information, reflecting, and choosing. So, . . . if beings are capable of making choices, we should, other things being equal, allow them to decide whether or not their lives are worth living. . . .

John Stuart Mill believed individuals should make their own decisions.

Anyone who values individual liberty should agree with Mill that the person whose life it is should be the one to decide if that life is worth continuing. . . .

Examining Physician-Assisted Suicide in the Real World

Undoubtedly, the most widely invoked secular argument against the legalization of voluntary euthanasia is the slippery-slope argument, i.e., that legalizing physician-assisted suicide or voluntary euthanasia will lead to vulnerable patients being pressured into consenting to physician-assisted suicide or voluntary euthanasia when they do not really want it. Or perhaps, as another version

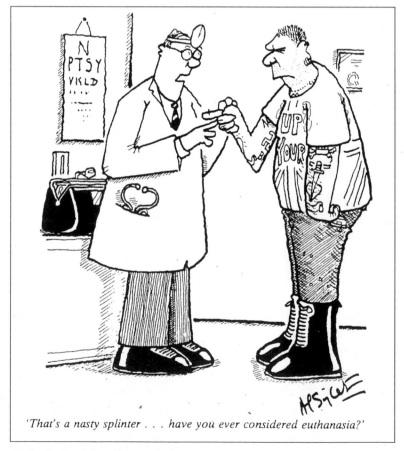

'That's a nasty splinter . . . have you ever considered euthanasia?'

AP Singler. Reproduced by permission.

of the argument goes, they will simply be killed without their consent, because they are a nuisance to their families or because their health-care provider wants to save money.

What evidence is there to support or oppose the slippery-slope argument when applied to voluntary euthanasia? A decade ago, this argument was largely speculative. Now, however, we can draw on evidence from several jurisdictions in which it has been possible for doctors to practice voluntary euthanasia or physician-assisted suicide without fear of prosecution. Active voluntary euthanasia has been openly practiced in the Netherlands since 1984, after a series of court decisions exonerated doctors who had been charged with assisting patients to die, and it was fully legalized by parliament in 1997. Belgium passed a similar law in 2002. Physician-assisted suicide—which allows the physician to prescribe a lethal dose of a drug, but not to give a lethal injection, has been legal in Switzerland for more than fifty years and in Oregon since 1997.

For Peace of Mind

There's no way to statistically measure peace of mind or quantify the death of terror. But here's a guess: For every one of the 91 terminally ill patients in Oregon who died with assistance from a physician, thousands have had their fears quieted just knowing such assistance would be there.

Betty Rollin, "Path to a Peaceful Death," *Washington Post*, May 30, 2004, p. B07.

No Abuse in Oregon

According to Oregon officials, between 1997, when the law permitting physician-assisted suicide took effect, and the end of 2004, 208 patients used the act to end their lives. The number of patients using the act increased during the first six years and fell slightly in the seventh, but the numbers are still very small. There are about 30,000 deaths in Oregon annually, and only about 1 in every 800 deaths in that state results from physician-assisted suicide. There have been no reports of the law being used to coerce patients to commit suicide against their will and no reports of abuses have reached the Oregon Board of Medical Examiners, which has formal responsibility to investigate complaints. Contrary to suggestions that in the United

States, physician-assisted suicide would be pushed upon those who are poor, less well-educated, and uninsured, Oregonians with a baccalaureate degree or higher were eight times more likely to make use of physician-assisted suicide than those without a high-school diploma, and all of those who have used the law to date have had some kind of health insurance. From all the available evidence, this does not appear to be a situation in which the law is being abused.

No Risk to Vulnerable People in the Netherlands

Opponents of voluntary euthanasia contend that the open practice of voluntary euthanasia in the Netherlands has led to abuse. In the early days of nonprosecution of doctors who carried out voluntary euthanasia, prior to full legalization, a government-initiated study known as the Remmelink Report indicated that physicians occasionally—in roughly 1,000 cases a year, or about 0.8 percent of all deaths—terminated the lives of their patients without their consent. This was, almost invariably, when the patients were very close to death and no longer capable of giving consent. Nevertheless, the report [and a similar study] . . . did not show any significant increase in the amount of nonvoluntary euthanasia happening in the Netherlands and thus dispelled fears that that country was sliding down a slippery slope. . . .

These studies discredit assertions that the open practice of active voluntary euthanasia in the Netherlands had led to an increase in nonvoluntary euthanasia. There is no evidence to support the claim that laws against physician-assisted suicide or voluntary euthanasia prevent harm to vulnerable people. Those who still seek to paint the situation in the Netherlands in dark colors now need to explain the fact that that country's neighbor, Belgium, has chosen to follow its lead. The Belgian parliament voted, by large margins in both the upper and lower houses, to allow doctors to act on a patient's request for assistance in dying.

Physician-Assisted Suicide in Europe

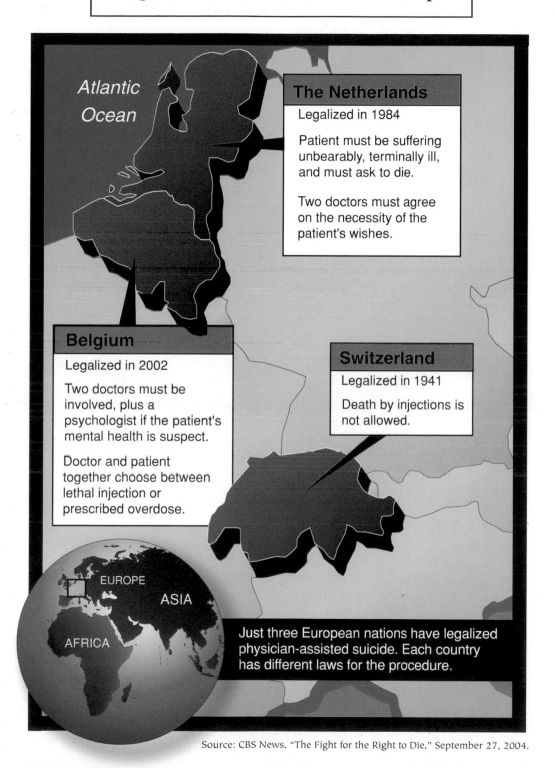

Atlantic Ocean

The Netherlands

Legalized in 1984

Patient must be suffering unbearably, terminally ill, and must ask to die.

Two doctors must agree on the necessity of the patient's wishes.

Belgium

Legalized in 2002

Two doctors must be involved, plus a psychologist if the patient's mental health is suspect.

Doctor and patient together choose between lethal injection or prescribed overdose.

Switzerland

Legalized in 1941

Death by injections is not allowed.

EUROPE
ASIA
AFRICA

Just three European nations have legalized physician-assisted suicide. Each country has different laws for the procedure.

Source: CBS News, "The Fight for the Right to Die," September 27, 2004.

Employees of a Swiss funeral service carry a casket from an assisted-suicide clinic where a terminally ill British man died in 2003.

The majority of Belgium's citizens speak Flemish, a language so close to Dutch that they have no difficulty in reading Dutch newspapers and books or watching Dutch television. If voluntary euthanasia in the Netherlands really were rife with abuses, why would the country that is better placed than all others to know what goes on in the Netherlands be keen to pass a similar law?

All People Deserve the Freedom to Control Their Lives

One way to interpret the results of the studies of euthanasia in Australia and Belgium, as compared with studies in the Netherlands, is that legalizing physician-assisted suicide or voluntary euthanasia brings the issue out into the open and thus makes it easier to scrutinize what is actually happening and to prevent harm to the vulnerable. If the burden of proof lies on those who defend a law that restricts individual liberty, then in the case of laws against physician-assisted suicide or voluntary euthanasia, that burden has not been discharged.

In jurisdictions where neither voluntary euthanasia nor physician-assisted suicide is legal, whether death comes sooner or later for terminally ill patients will often depend on whether or not they require a respirator which most physicians will be prepared to withdraw. Or it may vary with how ready a physician is to administer life-shortening doses of a painkiller, perhaps risking being reported to the police by a zealously pro-life nurse. Whether we are concerned to maximize liberty or to reduce suffering, we should prefer that the time when death comes depends on the wishes of mentally competent patients. The Netherlands, Belgium, Switzerland, and Oregon now allow their citizens or residents to make that decision. There is no sound reason why other countries, and other parts of the United States, should not allow their citizens the same freedom.

Analyze the essay:

1. Singer begins his essay with a well-known anecdote offered by the philosopher John Stuart Mill about people crossing a bridge. What is the meaning of this example? How does it pertain to physician-assisted suicide?

2. In this viewpoint the author argues that physician-assisted suicide should be legal on the grounds that people should have control over their own lives. The author of the next viewpoint argues against the practice on the grounds that people could be taken advantage of. After reading both viewpoints, which author do you agree with? Why?

Assisted Suicide Should Not Be Legal

Wesley J. Smith

In the following viewpoint Wesley J. Smith argues that physician-assisted suicide should not be legal because it is too dangerous. Smith claims that in Oregon, where physician-assisted suicide is legal, mentally unstable people have been allowed access to life-ending drugs even though they are not competent to make such a decision. He also argues that the law's supposed safeguards, such as the provision that eligible patients must be expected to die within six months of being issued a prescription for lethal drugs, have been violated. Smith concludes the practice should be illegal because the law does not offer adequate protection for vulnerable patients.

Wesley J. Smith is the author of the book *Culture of Death: The Destruction of Medical Ethics in America* and a frequent contributor to the *Weekly Standard*, from which this viewpoint was taken.

Consider the following questions:

1. According to Smith, who contributes to annual state reports about Oregon's assisted suicide law? Why does he object to this?
2. As described by Smith, how did Physicians for Compassionate Care help Michael P. Freeland?
3. What did one social worker find in Freeland's home, according to the author?

A paper presented at [the May 2004] American Psychiatric Association meeting demonstrates once again that the legalization of physician-assisted suicide in Oregon was one of the great public policy con jobs of all time. Earnest euthanasia advocates—generally abetted by a compliant media—spun the myth that assisted suicide would invariably be a rational "choice," strictly regulated by the state, a last resort of dying patients when nothing else could be done to alleviate their suffering. But the more we learn about how doctor-facilitated death is actually being practiced in Oregon, the clearer it becomes that these assurances were false.

Assisted Suicide Details Secret and Unscrutinized

Getting access to this information isn't easy. Assisted suicide in Oregon is shielded from meaningful public scrutiny by a shroud of state-imposed secrecy. As a consequence, little is publicly known about the people who have died by swallowing massive overdoses of toxic drugs prescribed by doctors. Indeed, the assisted suicide law was written and later interpreted by state regulators to ensure that the Oregon Health Department is powerless to control the practice of assisted suicide before patients die.

What little oversight the department imposes consists primarily of collecting and publishing data received after the fact. And almost all of the information collected and regurgitated by the state in annual reports comes from the doctors who do the lethal prescribing. In fact, the department is so incurious about the facts and circumstances surrounding assisted suicides, that even when it learns that a lethal prescription request was previously refused, no one calls the nonprescribing doctors to find out why. Nor do the "regulators" usually interview close friends and family members of the patient, who may have information about the patient's circumstances unknown to the prescribing doctor.

A Disturbing and Uncontrolled Industry

Still, here and there, disturbing information about the actual practice of assisted suicide in Oregon has trickled into the public domain. One such case came to light May 6 [2004], when psychiatrist N. Gregory Hamilton and his wife Catherine presented their paper to the psychiatrists' meeting, vividly demonstrating the dangers Oregon-style assisted suicide poses to incompetent and vulnerable patients. The Hamiltons are affiliated with Physicians for Compassionate Care, an Oregon-based medical association that supports providing better services to the dying and opposes assisted suicide.

Even though legalized assisted suicide has been practiced for more than six years, this is the first case in Oregon in which the patient's medical records have been made available for review. And a sorry tale they tell: Not only was the patient apparently not terminally ill as defined by Oregon's law when he first received his lethal prescription, but he was allowed to keep his cache of suicide pills despite being diagnosed as having "depressive disorder," "chronic adjustment disorder with depressed mood," "intermittent delirium," and even after being declared mentally incompetent by a court.

One Patient's Story

Michael P. Freeland was diagnosed with lung cancer in 2000. He received a lethal prescription from Dr. Peter Reagan in early 2001. Reagan is a committed suicide activist; euthanasia advocacy groups often refer suicidal patients to him when the patients' physicians refuse to go along with their requests for suicide drugs. In other words, Reagan regularly takes on patients solely for the purpose of facilitating their suicides.

Freeland, as it happens, died naturally on December 5, 2002. Oregon law requires the patient to be reasonably expected to die within six months before receiving a lethal prescription. But Freeland's death occurred nearly two years after Reagan wrote the lethal prescription. Indeed, Freeland told the Hamiltons that Reagan contacted him after he didn't die in a timely fashion to reissue the prescription to make sure his assisted suicide remained legal!

To receive a lethal prescription in Oregon, a patient must be expected to die within six months.

Depressed, Suicidal, and Mentally Unstable

On January 23, 2002, more than a year after receiving Reagan's poison script, Freeland was admitted to Providence Portland Medical Center for depression with suicidal and possibly homicidal thoughts. A social worker went to Freeland's home and found it "uninhabitable," with "heaps of clutter, rodent feces, ashes extending two feet from the fireplace into the living room, lack of food and heat, etc. Thirty-two firearms and thousands of rounds of ammunition were removed by the police." Amazingly, the "lethal medications" that had been prescribed more than a year before were left in the house—presumably in case Freeland wanted to use them.

Freeland was hospitalized for a week and then discharged on January 30. The discharging psychiatrist noted with approval that the guns had been removed, "which resolves the major safety issue," but wrote that Freeland's lethal prescription remained "safely at home." Freeland was permitted to keep the overdose even though the psychiatrist reported he would "remain vulnerable to periods of delirium." In-home care was considered likely to assist with this problem, but a January 24 chart notation noted that Freeman "does have his life-ending medications that he states he may or may not use, so that [in-home care] may or may not be a moot point."

> ## Depression Leads People to Ask for Assisted Suicide
>
> National studies show that among patients requesting assisted suicide, depression is the only factor that significantly predicts the request for death. Sixty-seven percent of suicides are because of psychiatric depression. By Oregon's fifth year, only 13% of suicide victims received psychiatric counseling.
>
> Oregon Right to Life, 5th Annual report, Oregon Dept. of Human Services, 2003.

Valuing Life over Death

The day after his discharge, the psychiatrist wrote a letter to the court in support of establishing a guardianship for Freeland, writing, "he is susceptible to periods of confusion and impaired judgment." According to the Hamiltons, the psychiatrist concluded that Freeland

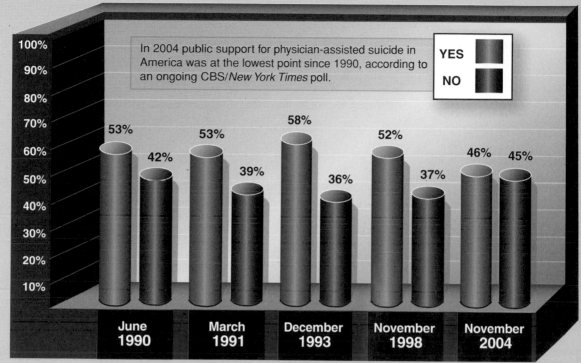

Declining Support for Physician-Assisted Suicide

In 2004 public support for physician-assisted suicide in America was at the lowest point since 1990, according to an ongoing CBS/*New York Times* poll.

YES
NO

100%
90%
80%
70%
60%
50%
40%
30%
20%
10%

53%   42%   53%   39%   58%   36%   52%   37%   46%   45%

June 1990   March 1991   December 1993   November 1998   November 2004

*Numbers may not add up to 100% because of rounding or alternate answers.
Source: CBS News/*New York Times*.

was unable to handle his own finances and that his cognitive impairments were unlikely to improve. He lived under supervision for a brief time, but was soon home alone with ready access to his suicide drugs.

Happily for Freeland, he had called Physicians for Compassionate Care for help, and as he neared his end, he had people surrounding him who were committed to helping him live his life rather than being committed to facilitating his death. Rather than dying alone by assisted suicide, he was instead cared for by the Hamiltons and by his friends—who assured the now imminently dying man "that they valued him and did not want him to kill himself."

Asay. © *Colorado Springs Gazette Telegraph*. Reproduced by permission.

Freeland was properly treated for depression with medication. He received good pain control, including a morphine pump. Best of all, he was reunited with his estranged daughter and died knowing she loved him and would cherish his memory. . . .

Assisted-Suicide Safeguards Are Inadequate

Assisted suicide advocates like to point to Oregon's law and declare that legally facilitated death there is well-managed. But the experiences of Michael Freeland and [others] demonstrate that Oregon's protective guidelines offer scant protection to vulnerable and depressed patients. Moreover, the meager safeguards that do exist evaporate once the lethal prescription has been issued, at which point no doctor is required to ensure that the patient remains competent, no doctor is required to be at the patient's bedside when the overdose is taken, and no one is responsible to ensure that patients are capable of understanding what they are doing when they actually take the lethal dose.

This leaves incompetent and vulnerable patients exposed to the worst potential abuses. Assisted suicide in Oregon isn't compassion: It is abandonment.

Analyze the essay:

1. Wesley J. Smith focuses on the story of Michael P. Freeland to illustrate why he believes physician-assisted suicide should be illegal. In your opinion, is this a compelling way to make his argument? Why or why not?

2. Smith argues that Oregon's physician-assisted suicide law is being abused. In the previous viewpoint, Peter Singer argues that the Oregon law is not being abused. What data does each author use to back up his claim? Which evidence do you find more compelling? Explain your answer.

Physician Aid in Dying Promotes Dignity and Autonomy

Compassion & Choices

The following viewpoint is a collection of stories published by Compassion & Choices, a pro–physician aid-in-dying organization. Each contributor describes the experience of a terminally ill loved one who either endured torturous incapacitation or resorted to desperate forms of suicide. The writers explain that although they try to remember their loved ones as they were in life, their memory is marred by the agonizing circumstances of their deaths. Physician aid in dying, they argue, could save many people from such fates and let them end their lives with dignity and control.

Compassion & Choices is a Colorado-based organization that advocates people's right to a full range of choices for dying with comfort, dignity, and control.

Consider the following questions:

1. How did Diane's father choose to deal with his lung cancer?
2. When did Max's friend choose to join the right-to-die movement? Why?
3. Describe the experiences of Jean's daughter, June, in the nursing home.

Diane's Story: A More Dignified Way

Today is Memorial Day. My dad was a veteran of World War II. He fought and lived through a terrible war, but when he found out he had lung cancer and emphysema, he fought a battle he knew he would lose. On June 4,

1991, he decided to end the war forever by ending his last battle.

He had taken 37 radiation treatments that had decreased the tumor in his lung so much it did not show up on x-rays in October '90. By March '91, the tumor was back and growing.

Dad was a very active person, as are most seniors. They grew up working hard and forgot how to take it easy.

Dad gave no indication the night before when I talked to him that he was thinking about taking his own life. Monday he went for his doctor's appointment. Tuesday and Wednesday he lay in the bed, too sick and weak to get up except to go to the bathroom, which was getting to be a chore for him.

Families Deserve More

Thursday, when I came home and fixed his supper to take to his room, I found him in his room with his head mostly blown off and blood and brain matter scattered all over his room and the hall to the bathroom. . . .

I am writing this to you today so that you can put this story in your newsletter or whatever publication you want so that others will not have to deal with the horrific sight that this kind of suicide causes. . . .

I hope that you can help others to realize that they and their families deserve a less horrible, more dignified way of dying. . . .

Max's Story: Suffering Cancer of the Tongue

Max was a very dear friend whom I try to remember the way he was in the early spring of 1998 . . . 51 years old, and glowing with the joy of life.

In late spring of 1998, Max was diagnosed with cancer of the tongue. The doctors said that if they excised his tongue, he might have a good chance for survival. So in early June, Max underwent the surgery, and about ten days later, he came home to start his new life. . . .

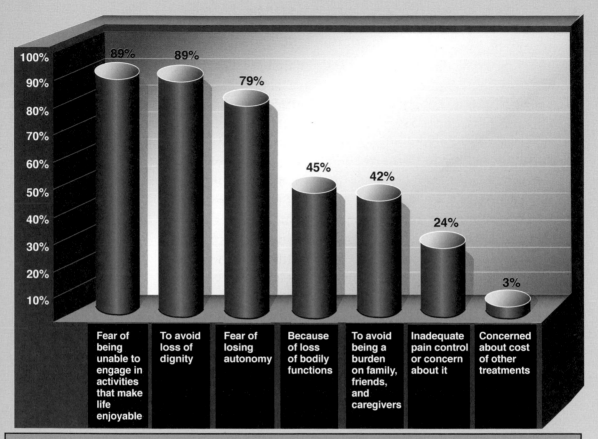

Reasons People Chose Physician-Assisted Suicide

Reason	Percentage
Fear of being unable to engage in activities that make life enjoyable	89%
To avoid loss of dignity	89%
Fear of losing autonomy	79%
Because of loss of bodily functions	45%
To avoid being a burden on family, friends, and caregivers	42%
Inadequate pain control or concern about it	24%
Concerned about cost of other treatments	3%

*Numbers only apply to Oregon and do not add up to 100% because respondents gave more than one answer.

Source: 8th Annual Report on Oregon's Death with Dignity Act, 2006.

See[ing] Max [after the surgery] was one of the most traumatic experiences of my life. The loss of his tongue, I learned, involved a great deal more than we had imagined. First, there was the permanent trache tube, to insure that he could breathe, and the insert had to be removed and cleaned each day. Then, there was the direct line into his intestine, through which Max had to feed himself liquid nutrients for 12 hours each day. And then, the worst problem by far . . . his inability to control salivation. . . .

Hell on Earth

The next visit I was fully prepared, and managed to maintain a cheerful demeanor. When I asked whether he was making progress with his swallowing exercises, he nodded a half-hearted affirmative, but it seemed that perhaps there was even more bothering him than I knew about . . . or perhaps it was only my imagination. Unfortunately, it wasn't.

In the subsequent weeks they found that Max was developing another, highly aggressive tumor in his throat. For whatever reason, further radiation was not considered an option. The tumor grew rapidly. They treated the physical pain, but that was the smallest part of Max's problem. Imagine, if you can, spending months sitting up in a chair, unable to lie down to sleep or rest, managing a cat-nap now and then, waking to connect another bottle of nutrients to your feeding tube, drooling huge globules into your bucket, while you waited patiently for the tumor in your throat to grow big enough to strangle you. It was hell on earth!

A Pitiful End for a Great Man

Max had about four months of that nightmare which some people insist upon calling "life." When death finally claimed him, my radiant 6'1", 185-pound friend was a pitiful 80-pound scarecrow.

The morning after delivering the eulogy at Max's funeral I joined the right-to-die movement. Ever since, I have devoted myself to the battle for legislation that will provide terminally ill patients with the means to avoid such horrific suffering. . . .

Death *Without* Dignity: Jean's Story

Ever since my youth I have proclaimed loudly that I'm not afraid of dying. Recently I realized how wrong I was; I'm not afraid of death, but I am afraid of dying. When we have a pet that is suffering, we take it to the vet to have it "put down." Even a murderer on Death Row gets a merciful death. Why must humans suffer when there is no hope of recovery? . . .

Protesters express their support for Oregon's physician-assisted suicide law during a 2005 demonstration.

Watching My Daughter Lose Control

On May 19th June, my oldest daughter at 71, had surgery for a brain tumor called glioblastoma multiforme (grade 4) a deadly malignancy with a prognosis of 4 to 6 months without treatment. Chemotherapy makes the patient so sick that the few extra months gained are not worth it. My daughter opted not to have treatment.

During the weeks she lived with me I made her life as easy as possible. However, when the Hospice nurse told her new tumors had developed on the back of her neck, she lost control. She began over-medicating, falling and hurting herself. Breaking my promise to her that she could stay with me until she died, we moved her into a nursing home. . . .

"Why Does It Take So Long?"

Overnight she became bedridden, able only to babble, frustrated because she couldn't express her thoughts. She slipped in and out of a coma. When we spoke to her she screwed up her face, crying without tears. She mumbled only two intelligible sentences during those weeks: "Why does it take so long?" and, "I didn't know it would be so hard."

Now we are praying for her to die. When the Hospice nurse suggested tube feeding because she wasn't eating, we said, "Absolutely not! She doesn't want to live." A morphine patch was placed on her chest to prevent pain. The strain on family members is almost unbearable; we can only stand by and watch her suffer. If we should try to help

BY TOLES FOR THE BUFFALO NEWS

Toles. © 1993 Distributed by Universal Press Syndicate. Reproduced by permission.

her die, we would be breaking the law and probably go to prison. June has a Living Will and a "Do Not Resuscitate" order. She expressed her wishes while she was still lucid, but that doesn't help us to help her. . . .

Let's Make It Easier

My 74-year-old father ended a miserable existence by climbing the George Washington Bridge and dropping over the side, to be smashed on the pavement. Nobody deserves such a death. Why couldn't he die peacefully with a doctor's help?

In the past several years California has tried to pass a law similar to Oregon's. The attempt failed, due to fears of euthanasia, etc. Don't these people who vote against the law realize that some day their loved ones—or they themselves—might welcome the release such a law can provide? No one should have to choose an end like my father's or my daughter's. Death is inevitable—let's make it easier for those who want help.

Analyze the essay:

1. Each of these stories includes specific, graphic details that aim to draw the reader in. Did you find these vivid details compelling? Did you empathize with the people in the stories? If so, why? If not, why not?

2. After reading this viewpoint and the next, what conclusions have you come to about whether physician aid in dying promotes dignity and autonomy? What evidence helped you make your decision?

Assisted Suicide Does Not Promote Dignity and Autonomy

Ron Amundson and Gayle Taira

In the following viewpoint authors Ron Amundson and Gayle Taira argue that physician-assisted suicide offers people neither dignity nor autonomy. Taira describes how she was permanently disabled in a car accident. While in the hospital, she overheard her nurses, the people she had entrusted with her life, discuss how they would kill themselves if they were her. Taira maintains that being disabled is not the equivalent of long death. She and Amundson argue that true dignity and autonomy are achieved when one lives life to its fullest rather than weakly opting for suicide.

Gayle Taira is a graduate student at the University of Stirling, Scotland. Ron Amundson is a professor of philosophy at the University of Hawaii at Hilo.

Consider the following questions:

1. What does the word *ableist* mean in the context of the viewpoint?
2. What meaning does the pro–assisted suicide slogan "Death with Dignity" have for the authors?
3. According to the article, what were the top three reasons given by people for requesting assisted suicide in Oregon in 2002?

[R on Amundson:] When [I first examined the issue of] assisted suicide [I noticed that when] advocates really wanted to scare their audience, they didn't use unremitting pain to do it. They used disability. The need for help to go to the toilet was the big stick. Wouldn't you rather die than have someone else wipe your butt? It never seemed to cross these advocates' minds that thousands of people in the United States get help to wipe their butts every day. Many of them are my friends. The blatant disdain and scorn that the assisted suicide advocates showed for people with real disabilities disgusted me. I began to see the smug slogan "Death with Dignity" in a new light: It hid the assumption that dignity was forever out of the reach of people who were disabled; "Better Dead than Disabled." . . .

A Life-Altering Accident

[Gayle Taira:] In September 1992, I was in an automobile accident. A drunk driver crossed the center line and crashed into my car. My passenger was killed. I received serious brain injuries, along with numerous broken bones and contusions. At first my condition was very frightening to those who knew me. I could barely recognize my family and could not remember anyone's name. My ability to speak was extremely limited because of aphasia, and my physical injuries made gesturing impossible. I was diagnosed with traumatic brain injury (TBI), a condition from which I am still recovering and with which I am learning to deal.

For many months after the accident I had trouble with both short-term and long-term memory. I had difficulty speaking and doing arithmetic. I had to learn how to read again. I also had a visual–spatial difficulty: I did not know where my body was, so I often remained quite still, not even gesturing. In the early days I had little concept of time, and 2 minutes was the same as 3 hours to me. As a consequence, from the "outside," it often looked as if there was nothing going on "inside" of me. . . .

Ten years later, I still have difficulty with certain language tasks. I can't hear myself speak, for instance, and I often get tenses mixed up. I have difficulty with prepositions. (I noticed this while taking a French language course.)

When I am tired, I have great difficulty in speaking. I have difficulty reading documents in certain fonts. Because of my visual–spatial difficulties I don't drive, and I don't cross busy streets or parking lots. I have learned to work with my impairments resulting from the TBI, and I have adjusted my lifestyle to let me do the things I want. . . .

The wreckage of a car crash offers a reminder of life and death issues.

"I'd Kill Myself if That Ever Happened to Me"

My approach to the physician-assisted suicide issue was completely changed by one single experience. It occurred right after my TBI and was the pivotal point in my interest in disability issues. In some sense it was an emotional reaction, but in another very real sense it was a philosophically reasoned change in view.

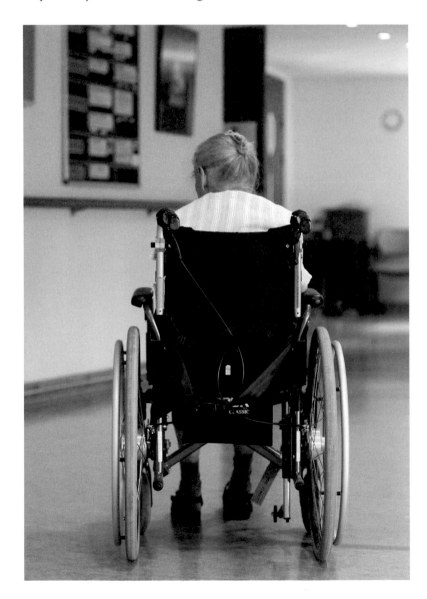

Some feel that ill or disabled people are incapable of making good decisions about their own well-being.

I was still in the hospital right after my automobile accident and sudden acquisition of TBI, going from one treatment center to another for innumerable tests. It is important to remember that TBI (and my inability to gesture) made it appear to some people that nothing was going on "inside" me. I found myself in a wheelchair in an elevator with two health care professionals. One woman was taking me to a set of medical tests. The other had joined us in the elevator. The first began to describe a car accident to the second person. She described the injuries, and the cognitive difficulties that occur with TBI. The other woman said, "You know, I'd kill myself if that ever happened to me. I don't want to end up like that."

They Believed I'd Be Better Off Dead

Like what? I wondered. Then I realized that they were talking about me, right then, right there. It was my accident she was describing, and the second woman would rather die than end up like me!

I suddenly realized (with a shock) that I had completely missed a crucial aspect of the physician-assisted suicide issue. I had incorrectly assumed that the individual making the choice would be free from coercion and would be making a choice based on his or her own interests, free from the forced perspective of others. I had assumed that the choices being offered were indeed legitimate choices. Talk about fatal assumptions! Sitting in the wheelchair in that elevator, I realized exactly how fatal that assumption is: The very people whose job it was to care for me believed that I would be better off dead, and I was powerless to argue against them. . . .

A Flawed Understanding of Dignity

The reports from Oregon of legalized assisted suicide for the year 2002 show that pain is not the primary reason for wanting to die—It's not even in the top three. Reports were solicited from physicians of the people who had requested assisted suicide about which of six reasons might have contributed to the request. The reported reasons were "losing autonomy (84%), decreasing ability to participate in activities that make life enjoyable (84%), and losing control of bodily functions (47%)." George Eighmey, executive director of the assisted-suicide advocacy group Compassion in Dying of Oregon, makes it clear that disability phobia is the primary cause for death wishes. "The No. 1 reason given to me is: 'I don't want to have anyone wipe my rear end.'" Given these statistics and public pronouncements, how could anyone maintain their self-respect and dignity and still be willing to live with a disability?

The typical arguments for assisted suicide are individualistic and personalized, based on the importance of individual choice over all else. They are flawed in two ways. First, they rely on the ableist prejudices of the audience: "Wouldn't you rather die than have someone else wipe your butt?" And second, the personalized form of the argument distracts the audience from recognizing that a social policy is being proposed. That policy amounts to a social endorsement of the correctness of certain suicide decisions, and we all know what those decisions are based on. Oregon has informed us: Ableist fear of disability, shame at needing help, dread of having someone else wipe one's butt. . . .

Dignity Is Found in the Strength to Live, Not the Wish to Die

We (the authors) have good news and bad news. The good news is that human beings are resilient. Young people often claim that they would rather die than get old. When they get old, they realize what fools they were when they were young. As oldsters, they are not obliged to commit suicide by their former lack of imagination about what makes life worth living. The same goes for acquiring a disability. It is possible for a person to create a perfectly delightful life under conditions that they never would have

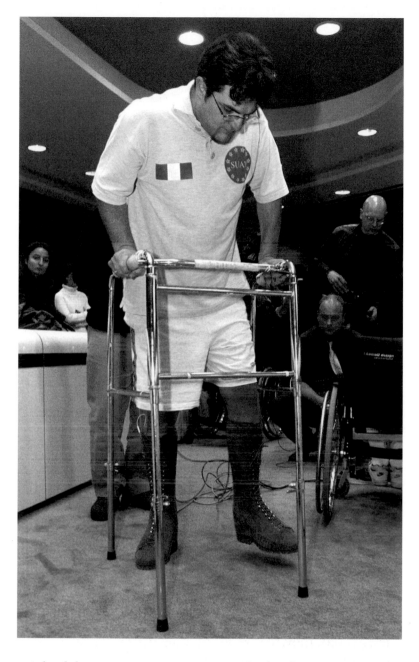

A paraplegic attempts to walk with the aid of electrodes secured to his legs.

wished for. Your previous, naive lack of imagination ("I would rather die than . . .") is no barrier to the quality of your new life.

The bad news is that far too many people fail to recognize their own resilience. In their ableist pridefulness, many people are convinced that death is better than the loss of (what amounts to) their self-image—even in so trivial a matter as the self-image of a do-it-yourself toilet user. This tragic short-sightedness can result in suicides. Even worse, it can result in a social policy that implicitly endorses such grounds for suicide.

Analyze the essay:
1. The authors lament that "too many people fail to recognize their own resilience." What do you think they mean by this assertion? Do you agree or disagree?
2. Both this viewpoint and the previous viewpoint are first-person narratives that focus on personal accounts and experiences. Consider the ways in which a first-person narrative affects the way you think about physician-assisted suicide. Does it make an aspect of the issue more compelling? If so, in what way? What are the weaknesses apparent in relying on personal stories, rather than statistical information, to form an opinion?

Assisted Suicide Decreases a Doctor's Commitment to Treat Patients

Physicians for Compassionate Care Educational Foundation

In the following viewpoint published by the Physicians for Compassionate Care Educational Foundation (PCCEF), the authors argue that physician-assisted suicide is incompatible with a doctor's role as a healer. Physicians are responsible for improving their patients' lives, not ending them, according to PCCEF. The authors conclude that patients should be able to trust that their doctors are making the best decisions for their health and not pushing them toward an early death.

Physicians for Compassionate Care Educational Foundation is an Oregon-based association of doctors and other health professionals who oppose physician-assisted suicide.

Consider the following questions:

1. According to PCCEF, what message is sent to patients when doctors write a prescription for lethal drugs?
2. How might depression influence a patient's request for physician-assisted suicide, according to the authors?
3. What does the word *incompatible* mean in the context of the viewpoint?

When the voters of Oregon approved the legalization of physician-assisted suicide in 1994,[1] many physicians in Oregon organized themselves into an organization called Physicians for Compassionate Care. As members of this organization we affirm an ethic that all human life is inherently valuable. We affirm that physicians' roles are to heal illness, alleviate suffering, and provide comfort for the sick and dying. We work to ensure appropriate care for our patients, to speak out for the inherent value of human life, and to uphold the time-honored values of our profession. We encourage physicians to: heal the patient; enhance support for patients who cannot be healed; avoid unnecessary therapies that will unduly prolong the dying process; educate health professionals and the public about the dangers of physician-assisted suicide and euthanasia, realizing that they are fundamentally incompatible with our role as healer. We encourage state of the art care for dying patients, including optimal pain management and the recognition and treatment of depression. We work to update health professionals on current pain management technology and palliative care for clinical use to help confront the challenges of serious, chronic and terminal illness with honesty, caring and commitment. We collaborate with other organizations to promote our mission.

The Duty and Role of Physicians

Physicians have the duty to safeguard human life, especially life of the most vulnerable: the sick, elderly, disabled, poor, ethnic minorities, and those whom society may consider the most unproductive and burdensome. Physicians are to use all knowledge, skills and compassion in caring for and supporting the patient. Medicine and physicians are not to intentionally cause death. The patient-physician trusting relationship is the most important asset of physicians and is for the protection of patients. . . .

1. Though voters first approved the act in 1994, due to legal injunction the act did not become law until 1997.

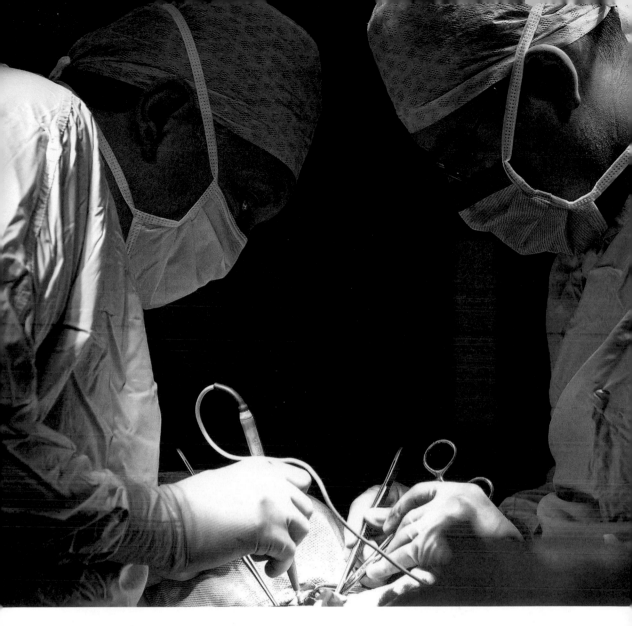

An Order to Die, the Power to Kill

The legalization of physician-assisted suicide does not give any new rights to patients. Its purpose is to legally protect doctors who write prescriptions for lethal drugs. Legalization of physician-assisted suicide takes away from terminally ill patients, the protection against doctors who order their death by a prescription for deadly drugs. Those who ask for a "right to die" have to give someone else the "power to kill". . . .

Surgeons (pictured) and other doctors must wrestle with ethical issues when patients are dying.

A prescription is a written order or directive to the patient. In physician-assisted suicide, a doctor writes a prescription for lethal drugs. . . . Physician-assisted suicide is really doctor-ordered, doctor prescribed, or doctor-directed suicide. When a doctor writes a prescription for physician-assisted suicide, the message to the patient is: your life is not worth living, you are better off dead, I don't value you or your life, I want you dead, I order you to die, I direct you to die. Those who desire a "right to die" are giving to doctors the "power to kill". Assisted suicide is fundamentally incompatible with the doctor's role as healer, comforter and consoler. Assisted suicide is the ultimate abandonment of a patient by a doctor. . . .

Doctors Are Supposed to Treat Patients

There is an inverse relationship between cancer patients, experience with pain and their favoring assisted suicide.

A DISPOSABLE SOCIETY

People with cancer are less in favor of assisted suicide than is the general public. Patients with pain want doctors to kill the pain, not kill the patient. We should focus on improving the care of patients, not on killing them.

In Oregon, only a small minority of patients dying of assisted suicide chose it because of fear of pain in the future. This was not because they were having pain. The proponents of assisted suicide acknowledge that pain is not an important reason for legalizing assisted suicide. The message that the proponents of assisted suicide are giving to the public and to patients, is that doctors can do a better job of killing patients than they can of caring for their medical needs. The doctors you don't trust

Doctors Should Not Snuff Out Life

In the name of compassion, doctors trained to heal and to prolong life are shortening and even snuffing it out altogether. Killing the patient as the cure is becoming an acceptable medical procedure in some circles.

Trudy Chun and Marian Wallace, "Euthanasia and Assisted Suicide: The Myth of Mercy Killing," *Concerned Women for America*, March 5, 2001.

to take care of you are going to be given the legal power to kill you. My patients have told me that they worry that the doctors will be the judge, jury and executioner of their lives.

Depression is the leading cause of suicide. There is a direct relationship between depression and favoring physician-assisted suicide. Depression is frequently overlooked in patients with serious physical illness. Depression needs to be diagnosed and properly treated with counseling and medications.

Physician-Assisted Suicide Destroys the Trust Between Patient and Doctor

The following is a personal story of Kenneth Stevens, M.D.: "We had been married for 18 years and had 6 children. For three years my wife had been suffering from advancing malignant lymphoma. It had spread from the lymph nodes to her brain, to her spinal cord and to her bones. She had received extensive chemotherapy and radiation treatments. She required considerable pain medication, antidepressants and other supportive measures. In late May, 1982, we met again with her physician to

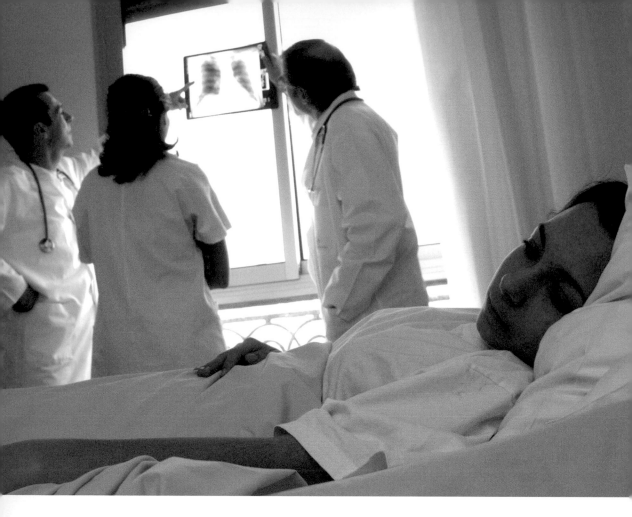

An ill patient waits for news from her doctors, who discuss her condition in the background.

review what more could be done. It was obvious that there was no further treatment that would halt the cancer's progressive nature. As we were about to leave his office, her physician said, "Well, I could write a prescription for an 'extra large' amount of pain medication for you." He did not say it was for her to hasten her death, but she and I both felt his intended message. We knew that was the intent of his words. We declined the prescription. As I helped her to our car, she said, "He wants me to kill myself." She and I were devastated. How could her trusted physician subtly suggest to her that she take her own life with lethal drugs? We had felt much discouragement during the prior three years, but not the deep despair that we felt at that time when her physician, her trusted physician, subtly suggested that suicide should be considered. His subtle message to her was, "Your life is no longer of value, you are better off dead." Six days later she died peacefully, naturally, with dignity and at ease in her bed, without the suggested lethal drugs. Physician-assisted suicide does destroy trust between patient and physician.

Analyze the essay:

1. How do the authors use the narrative technique in their essay? After identifying it, explain why you find this technique effective or ineffective.

2. The authors of this viewpoint are members of Physicians for Compassionate Care Educational Foundation, an anti-assisted suicide organization whose members are doctors. Does knowing that doctors wrote this viewpoint influence your opinion of it? If so, in what way?

Assisted Suicide Does Not Decrease Doctor's Commitment to Treat Patients

Wesley Sowers

In the following viewpoint psychiatrist Wesley Sowers argues that a doctor can both heal patients and help terminally ill patients end their lives without violating medical ethics. He points out that physician-assisted suicide is an option only when a patient's life is sure to end and pain and suffering have become unbearable. Doctors can show compassion for patients, Sowers believes, by helping make their last months as dignified and comfortable as possible. In this way, he concludes, doctors fulfill their roles as healers by helping patients preserve the meaning of their lives.

Wesley Sowers is medical director for the Office of Behavioral Health in the Department of Human Services for Allegheny County, Pennsylvania, and clinical associate professor of psychiatry at the University of Pittsburgh Medical Center.

Consider the following questions:

1. According to Sowers, what is the difference between suicide and assisted dying?
2. What safeguard prevents depressed people in Oregon from requesting physician-assisted suicide, as described by Sowers?
3. What does Sowers suggest physicians might offer the family members of patients who had chosen physician-assisted suicide?

Wesley Sowers, "Physician Aid in Dying and the Role of Psychiatry," *Psychiatric Times*, January 1, 2004, Copyright 2004 by CMP Media LLC, 600 Community Drive, Manhasset, NY 11030, USA. Reproduced by permission.

The debate over the rights of people who are near death to choose the time and circumstances of that final life passage has recently been revived . . .

Although physician involvement in this process is often referred to as physician-assisted suicide, I believe that this is a misnomer. Other descriptors, such as physician aid in dying or physician-assisted hastened death have often been dismissed as euphemisms. Nevertheless, there is an important distinction between these two concepts. Suicide signifies the premature, self-inflicted termination of a life that has not yet exhausted its potential. In the case of assisted dying, a person whose death is inevitable within a short period of time chooses the time and circumstances of their death. It is a considered rational response to avoid suffering associated with the meaningless extension of a life that has essentially reached its conclusion. In suicide, an individual engages in an act of emptiness and desperation arising from a perception that their existence lacks meaning. In assisted dying, the individual engages in a final act of fulfillment and resolution intended to preserve the meaning of their life and their identity as a person. . . .

Many Safeguards in Place to Prevent Abuse

It has been suggested that a decision by someone with terminal illness to hasten death is either the product of depression or may, in many cases, be coerced. Clearly, there may be cases in which people feel desperate and are depressed, and these conditions may lead them to suicidal behaviors. It is not difficult to determine when someone may be depressed, and the Oregon law and others like it require an assessment for depression whenever it is suspected. When adequate safeguards are in place, it is very unlikely that suicidal intentions will be overlooked and there have been no indications that this has been the case in the five years of practice in Oregon.

Concerns have also been raised that anxious relatives will encourage the hastening of death for their own benefit or that overzealous or overworked physicians will subtly coerce people with terminal illness to end their lives prematurely. Apart from being a depressingly cynical view of our society and profession, these scenarios have not occurred in Oregon and are also extremely unlikely under any laws with reasonable protections in place. Psychiatrists are frequently called upon to assess a person's capacity to make rational medical decisions, and the principles used for making these determinations should not be distinct from those employed to determine whether someone is capable of making decisions related to their time of death.

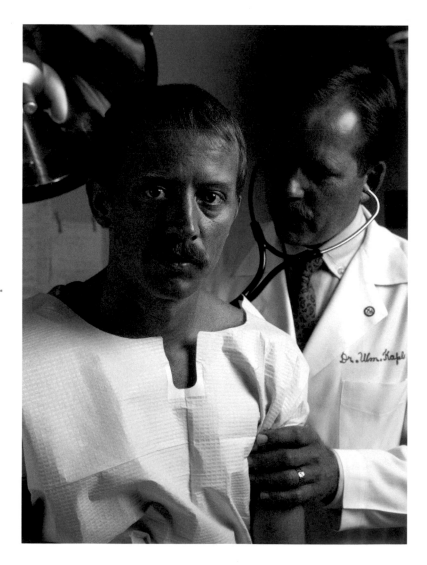

A physician examines an AIDS patient. Physicians can also offer comfort to patients with terminal conditions.

Doctors Can Offer Patients Dignity and Comfort

Some opponents of physician-aided dying believe that if palliative care were adequate, then there should be no need to hasten death. In Oregon, the primary reason that people have given for wishing to have this option has consistently been the fear of loss of autonomy and loss of control of bodily functions. While there is no question that palliative care sufficient to meet the needs of those who suffer must be broadly available, options such as terminal sedation or voluntarily stopping eating and drinking may not appeal to people who wish to have a dignified departure with a finite end that allows them to achieve closure in their lives.

One of the most commonly expressed concerns about legitimizing physician-assisted dying is the fear that it will open the door for more sinister practices such as state-sponsored euthanasia involuntarily applied to the disabled or otherwise devalued members of our society. While these concerns certainly deserve extreme vigilance, they are not supported by the experience in Oregon. They also run counter to the intent and base of support for physician-assisted dying. Involuntary euthanasia would deprive individuals of their right to life and choice, while physician-assisted dying attempts to support individual rights and is limited to those patients for whom death is inevitable and who demonstrate a consistent and well-considered desire to hasten that process. Those who support physician-assisted dying under these circumstances would, in most instances, strongly oppose coercion or involuntary forms of medicalized murder such as executions by injection.

It Is a Doctor's Job to Reduce Unnecessary Suffering

Physician involvement in cases of hastened death is appropriate because it is humane and respectful and allows

A woman discusses a family member's options with a doctor.

individuals to maintain their sense of value, their sense of purpose and their personal identity. Physicians have a responsibility to respect personal autonomy and support decision-making processes and choice. The absence of physician assistance does not reduce the prevalence of hastened death, but rather makes it a more difficult and unsupported process for those who choose it. Without choice and without the possibility of assistance, many people will become desperate, and it will be more likely that a violent, premature death will occur.

It is commonly asserted that assisting hastened dying is a violation of the Hippocratic Oath. Interpretations of the oath may vary and depend a great deal on translation, but if we address the most widely quoted directive of the oath—"First, do no harm"—we must recognize that the perception of harm can be quite variable. For someone who places extremely high value on the preservation of life in all situations, assisting death will be seen as a harmful act.

On the other hand, those who value autonomy, respect for individual choice and elimination of unnecessary suffering when death is imminent are likely to perceive more harm in withholding assistance. This is to say that the oath offers no clear direction on this issue. Individual physicians must use their own judgment and follow their conscience.

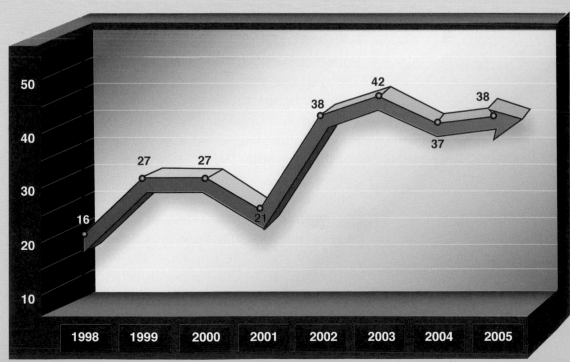

Number of Physician-Assisted Suicides in Oregon

16 — 1998
27 — 1999
27 — 2000
21 — 2001
38 — 2002
42 — 2003
37 — 2004
38 — 2005

Source: International Task Force on Euthanasia and Assisted Suicide.

An Irreplaceable and Supportive Role

Although critics of physician-aided dying argue that this practice will undermine public opinion of physicians, there is no evidence to support this claim. There is evidence, however, that the public would be respectful of physicians who would participate in requests for assistance in hastening death.

Many people question whether physicians are needed to help someone end their life and believe that other means are available should someone choose to hasten their death. They feel that physicians should remain aloof from this process to preserve their unique identity as healers. While it is true that other means are available, many will find comfort and feel supported through the aid of a physician.

Physicians may play an irreplaceable role in assisting family members and loved ones to understand an individual's decision and to help them play a supportive role when it is critically needed. These alone are adequate reasons to justify voluntary physician participation in hastening death.

Analyze the essay:

1. Sowers suggests that the term physician-assisted suicide should be replaced by phrases such as "physician aid in dying" or "physician-assisted hastened death." Why does he believe these word choices are important? In your opinion, how much does terminology affect your opinion of the procedure?

2. In this viewpoint Wesley Sowers argues that physician-assisted suicide does not violate the Hippocratic Oath, an oath by which doctors vow to dedicate themselves to enriching the lives of patients. In the previous viewpoint the authors argue the opposite. Do you think physician-assisted suicide conflicts with the Hippocratic Oath? Why?

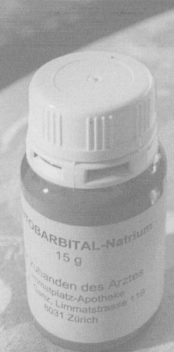

Section Two:
Model Essays
and Writing
Exercises

The Five-Paragraph Essay

An essay is a short piece of writing that discusses or analyzes one topic. The five-paragraph essay is a form commonly used in school assignments and tests. Every five-paragraph essay begins with an introduction, ends with a conclusion, and features three supporting paragraphs in the middle.

The Thesis Statement. The introduction includes the essay's thesis statement. The thesis statement presents the argument or point the author is trying to make about the topic. The essays in this book all have different thesis statements because each makes a different argument about assisted suicide.

The thesis statement should clearly tell the reader what the essay will be about. A focused thesis statement helps determine what will be in the essay; the subsequent paragraphs are spent developing and supporting its argument.

The Introduction. In addition to presenting the thesis statement, a well-written introductory paragraph captures the attention of the reader and explains why the topic being explored is important. It may provide the reader with background information on the subject matter or feature an anecdote that illustrates a point relevant to the topic. It could also present startling information that clarifies the point of the essay or put forth a contradictory position that the essay will refute. Further techniques for writing an introduction are found later in this section.

The Supporting Paragraphs. The introduction is then followed by three (or more) supporting paragraphs. These are the main body of the essay. Each paragraph presents and develops a subtopic that supports the essay's thesis statement. Each subtopic is then supported with its own facts, details, and examples. The writer can use various kinds of supporting material and details to back up the topic of each supporting paragraph. These may include statistics, quotations from people with special knowledge or expertise, historical facts, and anecdotes. A rule of writing is that specific and concrete examples are more convincing than vague, general, or unsupported assertions.

The Conclusion. The conclusion is the paragraph that closes the essay. Its function is to summarize or reiterate the main idea of the essay. It may recall an idea from the introduction or briefly examine the larger implications of the thesis. Because the conclusion is also the last chance a writer has to make an impression on the reader, it is important that it not simply repeat what has been presented elsewhere in the essay but close it in a clear, final, and memorable way.

Although the order of the essay's component paragraphs is important, the paragraphs do not have to be written in that order. Some writers like to decide on a thesis and write the introductory paragraph first. Other writers like to focus first on the body of the essay, and write the introduction and conclusion later.

Pitfalls to Avoid

When writing essays about controversial issues such as assisted suicide, it is important to remember that disputes over the material are common precisely because there are many different perspectives. Remember to state your arguments in careful and measured terms. Evaluate your topic fairly—avoid overstating negative qualities of one perspective or understating positive qualities of another. Use examples, facts, and details to support any assertions you make.

The Narrative Essay

Narrative writing is writing that tells a story or describes an event. Stories are something most people have been familiar with since childhood. When you describe what you did on your summer vacation, for example, you are telling a story. Newspaper reporters write stories of yesterday's events. Novelists write fictional stories about imagined events.

Stories are often found in essays meant to convince or persuade. The previous section of this book provided you with examples of essays on assisted suicide. All were essays that attempted to persuade the reader to support specific arguments about assisted suicide. In these essays, the authors, in addition to making assertions and marshalling evidence to support their points, also told stories about their experiences with assisted suicide. They were using narrative writing.

Components of Narrative Writing

All stories contain basic components of character, setting, and plot. These components answer four basic questions—who, when, where, and what—information readers need to make sense of the story being told.

Characters answer the question, Who is the story about? In a personal narrative using the first-person perspective ("My family helped my grandmother end her life"), the characters are the writer herself and the people she encounters. But writers can also tell the story of other people or characters ("Laurel Bergman helped her grandmother end her life") without being part of the story themselves. The setting answers the questions, When and where does the story take place? The more details given about characters and setting, the more the reader learns about them and the author's views toward them. Ron Amundson and Gayle Taira's second paragraph in Viewpoint Four and the first paragraph of Model Essay Two provide good examples of vividly describing the setting in which the stories take place.

The plot answers the question, What happens to the characters? Plot often involves conflict or obstacles that a story's character confronts and must somehow resolve. An example: Max's plot in Viewpoint Three revolves around his struggle with cancer of the tongue. The plot of Model Essay Three revolves around the narrator's struggle with her grandmother's failing health.

Some people distinguish narrative essays from stories in that essays have a point—a general observation, argument, or insight that the author wants to share with the reader. In other words, narrative essays also answer "why" questions: Why did these particular events happen to the character? Why is this story worth retelling? The story's point is the essay's thesis.

Using Narrative Writing in Persuasive Essays

Narrative writing can be used in persuasive essays in several different ways. Stories can be used in the introductory paragraph(s) to grab the reader's attention and to introduce the thesis. Stories can comprise all or part of the middle paragraphs that are used to support the thesis. They may even be used in concluding paragraphs as a way to restate and reinforce the essay's general point. Narrative essays may focus on one particular story or draw upon multiple stories.

A narrative story can also be used as one of several arguments or supporting points. Or, a narrative can take up an entire essay. Some stories are so powerful that by the time the reader reaches the end of the narrative, the author's main point is clear.

In the following section, you will read some model essays on assisted suicide that use narrative writing. You will also complete exercises that will help you write your own narrative essays.

Assisted Suicide: The Compassionate Choice

Editor's Notes As you read in Preface A in this section, narrative writing has several uses. Writers often incorporate the narrative technique into another type of essay, such as a persuasive essay or a compare-and-contrast essay. Instead of focusing their whole essay on a single story, they may use several different stories. They may also choose to use narration only in portions of their essay.

The following essay uses several different narrative stories to argue that assisted suicide is compassionate. As you read this essay, take note of its components and how it is organized. Also note that all sources are cited using MLA style. For more information on how to cite your sources, see Appendix C. In addition, consider the following questions:

1. How does the introduction engage the reader's attention?
2. How is narration used in the essay?
3. What purpose do the essay's quotes serve?
4. Would the essay be as effective if it contained only general arguments and omitted the stories of Jean's daughter and father?

Refers to thesis
and topic
sentences

Refers to
supporting
details

Paragraph 1

Every person must face death. Though each person's story is unique, end-of-life stories feature familiar characters and crises: the grandmother who loses her bout with breast cancer; the great-uncle whose heart finally gives out; the sister who succumbs to leukemia. Though all deaths are difficult, some are inordinately painful and drawn out. For those suffering people and their families, physician-assisted suicide could provide a compassionate end to difficult lives.

This is the essay's thesis statement. It clearly explains what the essay is about.

Paragraph 2

Assisted suicide allows people to avoid the unnecessary suffering that often accompanies the end of life. Consider the case of June, whose story is featured on the Compassion & Choices Web site. At the age of seventy-one, June developed a brain tumor that wreaked havoc on both her body and mind. She was unable to walk or move; confined to bed, she had to rely on nurses to keep her clean and to rotate her to avoid getting bedsores. She slipped in and out of a coma and lost the ability to speak coherently. During this time her mother, Jean, heard June say just two intelligible things: "Why does it take so long?" and "I didn't know it would be so hard." Assisted suicide would have saved both June and her mother from experiencing such a tortured death. June could have slipped away peacefully, avoiding the weeks of pain and immobility that marked the ending of her life. In fact, people who elect physician-assisted suicide in Oregon, where it is legal, do so for exactly these reasons. According to the Eighth Annual Report on Oregon's Death with Dignity Act, fear of losing personal dignity and autonomy, loss of control of bodily functions, and inadequate pain relief all ranked among the top six reasons why people preferred to die by physician-assisted suicide. As June's mother later reflected, "Even a murderer on Death Row gets a merciful death. Why must humans suffer when there is no hope of recovery?"

The story of June supports the essay's main point: Because some deaths are slow and painful, sufferers should have other options.

Citing evidence such as official studies or statistics lends hard support to the anecdotal evidence previously presented.

Well-placed quotes allow characters to speak for themselves.

Paragraph 3

Physician-assisted suicide is also compassionate because it gives people who are unwilling to endure an inevitably slow and painful death a dignified alternative to drastic, often violent, acts. Jean recounts how her father, who also suffered from a terminal illness, ended what she describes as "a miserable existence" by jumping off the George Washington Bridge. His body smashed into the pavement stories below, killing him instantly. Had physician-assisted suicide been available to him, however, he could have obtained a lethal prescription that would have allowed him

This is the topic sentence of the third paragraph.

to end his life peacefully. It would have spared him the pain of a violent suicide and saved his family from bearing the memory of how he died. People like Jean's father have been forced to resort to what author Peter Singer, who has written extensively on this issue, has termed "do-it-yourself (DIY) suicide." According to Singer, "People are determined to take control over the way in which they die and the timing of their death. In the absence of a change in the law [to legalize assisted suicide], DIY suicide is going to spread" (19). It seems logical that so long as people are intent on ending their lives, they might as well be provided with a way that is safe and peaceful.

Quoting from authorities can lend legitimacy to your essay.

Paragraph 4

This is the topic sentence of paragraph four.

Doctors can play a critical role in helping terminally ill patients end their lives with dignity and comfort. Though opponents of physician-assisted suicide argue that the procedure violates the Hippocratic Oath, by which doctors are sworn to "do no harm" to their patients, physician-assisted suicide is consistent with a doctor's obligation to relieve the suffering of their patients. When a patient is going to die anyway, how could it be wrong for a doctor to make sure his patient's life ends as comfortably as possible? As one British physician expresses it, "Do I believe in the concept of assisted euthanasia? Of course . . . as a doctor my job is to alleviate suffering" (27). Another physician puts the issue in the following way: "Those who value autonomy, respect for individual choice and elimination of unnecessary suffering when death is imminent are likely to perceive more harm in withholding assistance" than providing it, according to Wesley Sowers (37). In other words, for certain terminally ill patients whose last weeks or months are filled with pain and suffering, it is more compassionate for doctors to help them end their lives than to force them to remain alive in agony.

The author quotes from two doctors to make a point about physicians' role in assisted suicide. Always use sources that are relevant to your subject.

Transitional phrases such as "in other words" keep the ideas in the essay moving.

Paragraph 5

Death is never an easy thing to face, yet some deaths are made worse by prolonged suffering and anguish. In these cases, physician-assisted suicide should be made available to those who want to die in peace. Assisted suicide offers those who are very ill a chance to end their lives with dignity and control. To make such an option available would be the sign of a truly compassionate society.

The sentence concludes the essay by revisiting the main arguments made.

Works Cited

"Stories of Compassion and Choice." Compassion & Choices, 2005. < www.compassionandchoices.org. > .

Eighth Annual Report on Oregon's Death with Dignity Act, 2006. < www.oregon.gov/DHS/ph/pas/docs/year8.pdf > .

Singer, Peter. "Law Reform of DIY Suicide." *Free Inquiry* Feb.–Mar. 2005.

Sowers, Wesley. "Physician Aid in Dying and the Role of Psychiatry." *Psychiatric Times* 1 Jan. 2004.

Wilson, Libby, and Jim McBeth. "Do I believe in the concept of assisted euthanasia? Of course . . . as a doctor my job is to alleviate suffering." *Mail on Sunday (London)* 29 Jan. 2006.

Exercise A: Create an Outline from an Existing Essay

It often helps to create an outline for a five-paragraph essay before you write it. The outline can help you organize the information, arguments, and evidence you have gathered in your research.

For this exercise, create an outline that could have been used to write "Assisted Suicide: The Compassionate Choice." This "reverse engineering" exercise is meant to help familiarize you with how outlines classify and arrange information.

To do this you will need to

1. articulate the essay's thesis;
2. pinpoint important pieces of evidence;
3. flag quotes that supported the essay's ideas; and
4. identify key points that supported the argument.

Part of the outline has already been started to give you an idea of the assignment.

Outline

Write the essay's thesis:

I. Paragraph 2 Topic:

A. The story of June, who suffered a slow and painful death
B. Supporting evidence from the Eighth Annual Report on Oregon's Death with Dignity Act

II. Paragraph 3 Topic: Physician-assisted suicide prevents people from taking drastic and violent measures to avoid prolonged, painful deaths.

A.

B.

III. Paragraph 4 Topic:

A. Physician-assisted suicide is consistent with doctors'
   obligation to relieve the suffering of their patients.
   1. British physician's quotation

B.

   2.

Write the essay's conclusion:

Assisted Suicide Threatens the Disabled

■ Refers to thesis
  and topic
  sentences

■ Refers to
  supporting
  details

Editor's Notes The following narrative essay is different from the first model essay. Although it is still a five-paragraph essay, it makes its main point by focusing on one story instead of using small pieces of several different stories. However, that one story takes up most of the essay, not just one supporting paragraph. This is one model for writing a narrative essay.

The essay recounts the story of Kate Adamson-Klugman, who suffered a stroke that left her unable to move. The characters, setting, and plot are described in more detail than they would be in a simple anecdote to more strongly engage the reader in the story. In this way the author relies on the power of the story itself to make the essay's point that assisted suicide threatens the disabled.

The notes in the margins provide questions that will help you analyze how this essay is organized and written.

Paragraph 1

How does the introductory paragraph set up the story to come?

What is the essay's thesis statement?

One can imagine how Kate Adamson-Klugman began her day on June 29, 1995. Perhaps the athletic mother-of-two was thinking about the fitness-training business she was starting, or the success her husband, Steven, was enjoying as a lawyer. Perhaps she was contentedly viewing their beautiful five-bedroom California home, daydreaming about shopping lunches with friends. Yet on that June morning, Kate unexpectedly collapsed. As she was getting dressed after a shower, she felt her left side give way. She stumbled toward her husband, still asleep in bed. She tried to scream but all she could manage was a frantic mangle of unintelligible sounds. At the age of thirty-three Kate had suffered a devastating stroke. For the next ten weeks she hovered between life and death, and many of the doctors and nurses entrusted with her care did not believe she would survive. Her story is important because it reminds us that assisted suicide laws threaten the disabled and discourage them from fighting for their lives.

Paragraph 2

After her stroke Kate developed locked-in syndrome, one of the rarest and most feared consequences of a stroke. She could think, feel, and hear what was going on around her, but was unable to move, speak, or communicate in any way. She remembers, "I could do nothing. I was totally trapped in my body screaming, silently, helplessly." According to author David Hunt, "It was one of the most severe strokes her doctors had ever seen. It was a tragic case, a surgeon said at the time. Death would be a blessing." Another doctor suggested that Kate's husband contact a funeral home to make arrangements for his wife's remains (Genello 3). As expressed by another disabled person in such a situation, "The very people whose job it was to care for me believed that I would be better off dead, and I was powerless to argue against them." (Amundson and Taira 53). Because Kate was so thoroughly unresponsive, her doctors assumed she could not feel pain, and so inserted feeding tubes and other medical devices in her without using high levels of anesthesia. But Kate remembers feeling "every cut, every second" (qtd. in Crane 17). At one point her feeding tube was turned off for eight days. She had never imagined such a horrible hunger. She recalls, "I was in excruciating pain, in silence. I was on the inside screaming out: 'I do not want to die. Don't starve me. I want to live, feed me something!'" (qtd. in Crane 17).

Who is quoted in this paragraph? What purpose do these quotes serve?

This quote is taken from Viewpoint 4 in Section I. Take care to quote your sources accurately and cite them properly.

Paragraph 3

Thankfully Kate's family did not give up on her. Her husband, Steven, remained convinced that his wife was not lost and became determined to find a way to communicate with her. One day he asked her to blink her eyes if she could hear him. "It took all her energy to make it happen, but somehow [Kate] found the strength to do it—she blinked" (Hunt). Together they devised a system of

Paragraph three contains the essay's pivotal event.

communication. Steven would show her a board with the alphabet written on it; Kate would spell out words by blinking when he moved over the letter she wanted to use. The first word she spelled out was "home." Kate remembers, "Blinking for me was a landmark of epic proportions. It allowed me to let people know that I indeed was in there" (Adamson).

Paragraph 4

What transitional phrases are used in paragraph 4?

Slowly Kate's abilities began to return, though not without hard work. She had to wear a diaper because she did not initially have control over her body functions. In fact, she had lost the ability to do things that most of us take for granted, like eating, drinking, speaking, talking, and writing. But Kate eventually made a remarkable recovery. Though she remains paralyzed on her left side and wears a leg brace to help her walk, she is able to be a wife and mother and has an active and fulfilling career as a writer and speaker.

Paragraph 5

What is the topic sentence of this paragraph? How did you identify it?

How does the author switch from telling Kate's story to making a broader point about assisted suicide?

Kate Adamson-Klugman is a prime example of why assisted-suicide laws threaten the disabled. She easily could have been written off as a "vegetable" and relatives may have felt compelled to take advantage of an assisted-suicide law in a well-meaning attempt to end her suffering. Perhaps even Kate, in her darkest, weakest moment, would have given up and blinked "OK" had enough people around her convinced her that she was better dead than disabled. Assisted-suicide laws send the message to disabled people that they are a burden and their lives are not worth fighting for. Without such laws, however, people are encouraged to fight for their lives. Everyone deserves the chance to make as remarkable a recovery as Kate Adamson-Klugman. As she says, "The disabled, the helpless, the sick, and the elderly do not want special treatment. They just want to be treated as human beings" (qtd. Shibler 28). It is cases such as Kate's that speak strongly against adopting assisted-suicide laws.

Works Cited

Adamson, Kate. "A Stroke Survivor's Road to Recovery." <www.katesjourney.com>.

Crane, Anita. "Kate Adamson: A Voice for the Voiceless." *Celebrate Life,* July–Aug. 2005: 16–18.

Genello, William. "Defending All Life." *Catholic Light* 9 Feb. 2005: 3.

Hunt, David. "Kate's Journey." *South Bay Health* Mar.–Apr. 2005.

Interview of Kate Adamson-Klugman and Steven Klugman by Ann V. Shibler. "Defying the Death Culture." *New American* 16 May 2005.

Testimony of Kate Adamson before the U.S. House of Representatives Committee on Government Reform, Subcommittee on Criminal Justice, Drug Policy, and Human Resources. 19 Apr. 2005. <www.Katesjourney.com/041905-testimony.html>.

Exercise A: Create an Outline from an Existing Essay

As you did for the first model essay in this section, create an outline that could have been used to write "Assisted Suicide Threatens the Disabled." Be sure to identify the essay's thesis statement, its supporting ideas, and key pieces of evidence that were used.

Exercise B: Identify and Organize Components of the Narrative Essay

As you read in the section preface, narratives all contain certain elements, including setting, characters, and plot. This exercise will help you identify these elements and place them in order in your paragraphs.

In this exercise you will isolate and identify the components of a narrative essay. Viewpoint Four from Section One of this book is a good source to practice on, or you can find stories from another source. You may also, if you choose, use experiences from your own life or that of your family and friends.

Isolate and write down story elements.

Setting
The setting of a story is the time and place the main body of the story happens. Such information helps orient the reader. Does the story take place in the distant or recent past? Does it take place in a typical American community or exotic locale?

Essay Two	Story taken from this volume	Story from personal experience
California home and hospital June 29, 1995		

Character

Who is the story about? If there is more than one character, how are they related? At what stage of life are they?
What are their aspirations and hopes? What makes them
distinctive/interesting to the reader?

Essay Two	Story taken from this volume	Story from personal experience
Kate Adamson-Klugman, wife and mother who suffers an unexpected stroke		
Steven Klugman, husband who won't give up on his wife's recovery		
Doctors and nurses who do not believe their patient is capable of recovering from her stroke		

Pivotal Event

Most stories contain at least one single, discrete event on
which the narrative hinges. It can be a turning point that
changes lives or a specific time when a character confronts a challenge, comes to a flash of understanding, or
resolves a conflict.

Essay Two	Story taken from this volume	Story from personal experience
Kate manages to communicate with her husband by blinking, showing those around her she is aware and thinking in her unresponsive body.		

Events/Actions Leading Up to the Pivotal Event

What happens to the characters? What actions do the characters take? These elements are usually told in chronological order in a way that advances the plot—that is, each event proceeds naturally and logically from the preceding one.

Essay Two	Story taken from this volume	Story from personal experience
Despite living an active, healthy, and successful life, Kate Adamson-Klugman suffers an unexpected stroke. The stroke leaves her with locked-in syndrome, making her appear unresponsive and mentally dead.		

Events/Actions That Stem from the Pivotal Event

What events/actions are the results of the pivotal event in the story? How are the lives of the characters of the story changed?

Essay Two	Story taken from this volume	Story from personal experience
Kate manages a remarkable recovery, regaining nearly all her physical and cognitive abilities. Steven is credited with saving his wife's life by never giving in to ideas that she would never recover.		

The doctors and nurses who did not believe Kate could live learned that unresponsive patients can be mentally present.		

Point/Moral

What is the reason for telling the story? Stories generally have a lesson or purpose that is ultimately clear to the reader, whether the point is made explicitly or implied. Stories can serve as specific examples of a general social problem. They can be teaching tools describing behavior and actions that the reader should either avoid or emulate.

Essay Two	Story taken from this volume	Story from personal experience
The story illustrates why assisted-suicide laws could undermine a disabled person's will to live or make others act on instincts to end the patient's suffering.		

Memories of My Grandmother

Editor's Notes Essays drawn from memories or personal experiences are called personal narratives. The following essay is this type of narrative. It is not based on research or the retelling of someone else's experiences, such as the other narrative essays you have read in this book. Instead, this essay consists of an autobiographical story that recounts the writer's memories of an event involving assisted suicide. The essay differs from the first two model essays in that it is written from the subjective or first-person ("I") point of view. It is also different in that it is longer than five paragraphs. To be adequately developed, many ideas require more than five paragraphs. Moreover, the ability to write a sustained paper is a valuable skill. Learning how to develop a longer piece of writing gives you the tools you will need to advance academically. Many colleges, universities, and academic programs require candidates to submit a personal narrative as part of the application process.

As you read the following essay, take note of the sidebars in the margin. Pay attention to how points are organized and presented.

Refers to thesis and topic sentences

Refers to supporting details

"**B**arbara??" The terrified, whiny voice on the other end of the phone could only belong to one person.

"Hi Grandma, it's me," I said.

"Who is this? I want to talk to Barbara!"

"Mom's not here right now Grandma—it's Karen. You can talk to me."

"Karen? I don't know any Karen." Her voice became frantic and cracked. "I want to talk to Barbara! Where's Barbara?!"

"I'm your granddaughter. Barbara is your daughter."

"Who?"

Why do you think the writer chose to open the story with this dialogue? What mood does it set?

When I think of my Grandma Sondra, I have to forget certain moments of the last six months of her life. Moments when she did not know who I was, who she was, and did not know or feel anything but pain, fear, and confusion. If I erase those moments, I am left with memories of a sweet, caring, story-telling, cookie-making grandmother. How she used to get up at 5 A.M. to make coffee and read, waiting for my sister and me to wake up so we would play Scrabble with her. In those memories, she remains a solid figure of strength, wisdom, and comfort. It is a portrait I cherish, one that thankfully was only a little tainted by how sick she became at the end of her life. Had my mother and I not acted, however, the end of her life might have been much uglier and more difficult for all of us, most of all her, to bear.

My grandmother suffered from a brain tumor that slowly stole her away from us. In the morning she might call to ask me what was new with school, how my sister was handling her appointment as captain of the basketball team. Hours later she would call back, but not know who I was. Her doctors explained that the tumor was positioned in such a way that it made my grandmother prone to such episodes of panic and confusion. For all of us, it was extremely difficult to watch her slip in and out of reality.

One Saturday my mother and I went to visit her in her apartment in Manhattan. She lived on First Avenue, high above the noise and lights of Stuyvesant Town on the East Side. From her small windows we could see Gramercy Park, the East River, and on a clear day, all the way to Brooklyn. As the oldest, it was my treasured responsibility to get my grandmother Italian sodas and fresh bialys from the deli on the corner. I loved going to her apartment.

On this particular Saturday, though, my mother and I met a scene of complete disarray. The apartment was grossly neglected; unwashed dishes were stacked high in the sink, with rotting food encrusted on them. Heaps of dirty clothes around the bathroom and the bedroom emitted a foul stench. We found my grandmother in the back bedroom, exhausted and unable to care for herself. But she was lucid, today, at least.

As you read, consider how this essay uses narrative to make an argument about assisted suicide. How is this method different from a non-narrative pro–assisted suicide essay?

How is foreshadowing used in this paragraph? What purpose does it serve?

What have you learned so far about the characters? Do you care about them?

Notice how using particular details helps the scene come to life.

"Mom, you can't live like this anymore," said my mother. "We've got to get you help. You need someone to do the dishes, the laundry . . . ," she trailed off, her eyes wandering around the apartment at all that needed to be done.

"I won't have it," said Grandma defiantly. "I have never depended on anyone in my life and I won't start now."

"But Grandma," I said.

"Enough of this talk. Listen, girls," she sat up in her bed. My mother flinched, perhaps uncomfortable being called a girl, but deferred to her mother's authority. My grandmother took a deep breath and looked us straight in the eye. "I have a favor to ask of you. You're not going to like it, but I need you to listen and take what I am saying seriously. And I need you to say 'yes.'"

Note how the dialogue between the characters sounds natural and realistic. Can you picture them having this conversation?

We looked at each other, back at her, and nodded.

Cautiously, I said, "OK, Grandma. What is it?"

"Yesterday I found myself standing downstairs by the garbage chute, not knowing how I got there. This happens to me so often. I don't remember things. I am in pain, always." She paused and looked around the apartment. "Look at this mess. But I can only see it sometimes. I . . . I do need help. But what for? So I can extend this misery? So I can get further and further from the person I used to be? The person you know as your mother, as your grandmother? I am on the verge of being an enormous burden to all of you—and I won't have it."

Then she asked us in no uncertain terms to do something drastic: to help her end her life. Above our protests she made her case.

"Please. This is my wish. I don't want to wither away to a body that needs to be turned and wiped, getting nothing out of life and giving nothing to the people around me. There is only going to be more of this. More falling, more forgetting, more pain, more incontinence. Please. Help me to end my life in control, with resolution. It is what I want."

So my mother and I agreed to help, despite the risks. After all, helping someone commit suicide is against the law, and for good reason. But how could we deny my grandmother this ultimate request? Who were we to con-

A person's internal thoughts can help reveal what the character decides to do and why.

demn her to an eroding memory and a degraded sense of self? At the heart of her request was that she be allowed to end her life on her own terms, as herself, instead of suffering the indignity of not even recognizing her family members crowded around her bedside. My mother and I figured it was our duty to oblige her request. We too wanted to say good-bye to this beloved matriarch and have her really hear us, rather than watching her body outlive her mind. We therefore made a cocktail of lethal medication that would bring her the peaceful, dignified death she sought.

She didn't take it, at first. And for a couple weeks she seemed . . . lighter somehow, more positive. It was a welcome change, and at first I thought she might be making a miraculous recovery. But then I realized she was greatly comforted by the ability to once again direct her own life. The phone calls ceased. We even got a few more games of Scrabble in. But she must have seen a window closing. So after a Saturday visit from my mother, my sister, and me, she chose to close her life on a calm and dignified note. Bialys and Italian soda were her last delicious meal.

At her funeral I played her favorite sonata on flute, and read a piece that reflected on her life as a radical, an immigrant, a Holocaust survivor. There would be no more frantic phone calls in the middle of the night, no more watching her wither away to a shadow of a person. There would just be the memory of my grandmother, standing over the coffee pot at 5 in the morning, asking me if I wanted to play Scrabble.

Recurring details serve to develop the characters and plot. What recurring details were used in this essay? What effects did they achieve?

Why do you think the writer purposely depicts her grandmother as a strong person? What bearing does that have on the essay's point about assisted suicide?

Exercise A: Practice Writing a Scene with Dialogue

The previous model essay used scene and dialogue to make a point. For this exercise, you will practice creative writing techniques to draft a one- or two-paragraph scene with dialogue. First take another look at Essay Three and examine how dialogue is used.

When writing dialogue, it is important to:

1. Use natural-sounding language.
2. Include a few details showing character gestures and expressions as they speak.
3. Avoid overuse of speaker tags with modifiers, such as "he said stupidly," "she muttered softly," "I shouted angrily," and so on.
4. Indent and create a new paragraph when speakers change.
5. Place quotation marks at the beginning of and at the end of a character's speech. Do not enclose each sentence of a speech in quotation marks.

Scene-Writing Practice

Interview a classmate, friend, or family member. Focus on a specific question that pertains to assisted suicide, such as

- What would you do if you were terminally ill?
- What is your opinion of assisted suicide?
- Have you ever had to put a pet to sleep because it was suffering? What did you think of this experience? Should this practice be applied to humans? If so, with what parameters (rules)?
- Have you ever known someone who would have benefited from assisted suicide? Have you ever known someone who would have been at a disadvantage had assisted suicide been legal?
- Do you think people should have the right to die?

Take notes while you interview your subject. Write down what he or she says as well as any details that are provided. Ask probing questions that reveal the subject's feelings, words, and actions. Use your notes to create a brief one- or two-paragraph scene with dialogue.

But I Can't Write That

One aspect about personal narrative writing is that you are revealing to the reader something about yourself. Many people enjoy this part of writing. Others are not so sure about sharing their personal stories—especially if they reveal something embarrassing or something that could get them in trouble. In these cases, what are your options?

✔ Talk with your teacher about your concerns. Will this narrative be shared in class? Can the teacher pledge confidentiality?

✔ Change the story from being about yourself to a story about a friend. This will involve writing in the third person rather than the first person.

✔ Change a few identifying details and names to disguise characters and settings.

✔ Pick a different topic or thesis that you do not mind sharing.

Write Your Own Narrative Five-Paragraph Essay

Using the information from this book, write your own five-paragraph narrative essay that deals with assisted suicide. You can use the resources in this book for information about assisted suicide and how to structure a narrative essay.

The following steps are suggestions on how to get started.

Step One: Choose your topic.
The first step is to decide what topic to write your narrative essay on. Is there any subject that particularly fascinates you? Is there an issue you strongly support or feel strongly against? Is there a topic you feel personally connected to? Ask yourself such questions before selecting your essay topic. Refer to Appendix D: Sample Essay Topics if you need help selecting a topic.

Step Two: Write down questions and answers about the topic.
Before you begin writing, you will need to think carefully about what ideas your essay will contain. This is a process known as *brainstorming*. Brainstorming involves asking yourself questions and coming up with ideas to discuss in your essay. Possible questions that will help you with the brainstorming process include:

- Why is this topic important?
- Why should people be interested in this topic?
- How can I make this essay interesting to the reader?
- What question am I going to address in this paragraph or essay?
- What facts, ideas, or quotes can I use to support the answer to my question?

Questions especially for narrative essays include:

- Have I chosen a compelling story to examine?
- Does the story support my thesis statement?
- What qualities do my characters have? Are they interesting?

- Does my narrative essay have a clear beginning, middle, and end?
- Does my essay evoke a particular emotion or response from the reader?

Step Three: Gather facts, ideas, and anecdotes related to your topic.

This book contains several places to find information, including the viewpoints and the appendices. In addition, you may want to research the books, articles, and Web sites listed in Section Three or do additional research in your local library. You can also conduct interviews if you know someone who has a compelling story that would fit well in your essay.

Step Four: Develop a workable thesis statement.

Use what you have written down in Steps Two and Three to help you articulate the main point or argument you want to make in your essay. It should be expressed in a clear sentence and make an arguable or supportable point.

Examples:

Physicians are obligated to defend life at any cost—and this means never assisting with suicide.

(This could be the thesis statement of a narrative essay that examines various doctors' responses to requests that they assist with suicide.)

I had to face the terrible truth that my grandfather was going to die—whether or not I fulfilled his request to help him.

(This could be the thesis statement of a narrative essay in which a character debates whether to help a relative commit suicide.)

Step Five: Write an outline or diagram.

1. Write the thesis statement at the top of the outline.
2. Write roman numerals I, II, and III on the left side of the page with A, B, and C under each numeral.
3. Next to each roman numeral, write down the best ideas you came up with in Step Three. These

should all directly relate to and support the thesis statement.

4. Next to each letter write down information that supports that particular idea.

Step Six: Write the three supporting paragraphs.
Use your outline to write the three supporting paragraphs. Write down the main idea of each paragraph in sentence form. Do the same thing for the supporting points of information. Each sentence should support the paragraph of the topic. Be sure you have relevant and interesting details, facts, and quotes. Use transitions when you move from idea to idea to keep the text fluid and smooth. Sometimes, although not always, paragraphs can include a concluding or summary sentence that restates the paragraph's argument.

Step Seven: Write the introduction and conclusion.
See Preface A for information on writing introductions and conclusions.

Step Eight: Read and rewrite.
As you read, check your essay for the following:

- ✔ Does the essay maintain a consistent tone?
- ✔ Do all paragraphs reinforce your general thesis?
- ✔ Do all paragraphs flow from one to the other? Do you need to add transition words or phrases?
- ✔ Have you quoted from reliable, authoritative, and interesting sources?
- ✔ Is there a sense of progression throughout the essay?
- ✔ Does the essay get bogged down in too much detail or irrelevant material?
- ✔ Does your introduction grab the reader's attention?
- ✔ Does your conclusion reflect back on any previously discussed material or give the essay a sense of closure?
- ✔ Are there any spelling or grammatical errors?

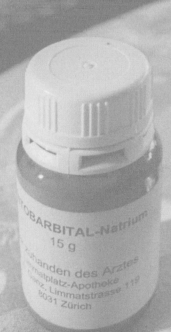

Section Three: Supporting Research Material

Facts About Assisted Suicide

Editor's Note: These facts can be used in reports or papers to reinforce or add credibility when making important points or claims.

Assisted Suicide in the United States

- Oregon is the only state in the United States where physician-assisted suicide is legal.

To be eligible for physician-assisted suicide under Oregon's Death with Dignity Act, a patient must be

- eighteen years of age or older
- an Oregon resident
- able to make and communicate his or her own health care decisions
- diagnosed with a terminal illness with six months or less to live

The law further requires that

- the patient make two verbal requests for assistance—separated by fifteen days—to a physician
- the patient's request be witnessed by two individuals who are not primary caregivers or family members
- the patient be able to rescind the verbal and written requests at any time
- the patient be able to self-administer the prescription
- the attending physician must be Oregon-licensed
- the diagnosis must be certified by a consulting physician, who must also certify that the patient is mentally competent to make health care decisions
- if either physician determines that the patient's judgment is impaired, the patient must be referred for a psychological examination

- the attending physician must inform the patient of alternatives, including palliative care, hospice, and pain management options
- the attending physician must request that the patient notify next-of-kin of the prescription request

According to the Eighth Annual Report on Oregon's Death with Dignity Act, published by the state of Oregon:

246 people have elected to die by physician-assisted suicide since the practice became legal in 1997.
- 16 in 1998
- 27 in 1999
- 27 in 2000
- 21 in 2001
- 38 in 2002
- 42 in 2003
- 37 in 2004
- 38 in 2005

The top five reasons given by patients who elected physician-assisted suicide in 2005 were:

1. Fear of decreasing ability to do enjoyable activities
2. Fear of loss of dignity
3. Fear of losing autonomy
4. Fear of losing control of bodily functions
5. Fear of being a burden

In 2005, sixty-four lethal prescriptions were written by doctors for patients who wished to die. By the end of the year, thirty-eight of the patients had taken the lethal medicine.

Oregonians who elected physician-assisted suicide most commonly suffer from the following illnesses:

- Lung and bronchus cancer
- Breast cancer
- Pancreas cancer
- Colon cancer
- Prostate cancer

- Ovarian cancer
- Skin cancer
- HIV/AIDS

Of the 246 people who have elected physician-assisted suicide since it became legal:

SEX
- 131 were male
- 115 were female

AGE
- 10 were 18–44
- 71 were 45–64
- 144 were 65–84
- 21 were 85 +

RACE
- 239 were white
- 6 were Asian
- 1 was Native American

Assisted Suicide Around the World

According to AssistedSuicide.org:
- Only four places in the world openly and legally allow physician-assisted suicide:
    1. Oregon (since 1997)
    2. Switzerland (since 1941)
    3. Belgium (since 2002)
    4. Netherlands (since 2002)
- Finland, France, Denmark, and Germany do not specifically ban assisted suicide.
- Norway has criminal sanctions against assisted suicide by using the charge "accessory to murder."
- In Italy the action is legally forbidden, although pro-euthanasia activists in Turin and Rome are pressing hard for law reform.
- Luxembourg does not forbid assistance in suicide because suicide itself is not a crime.
- In Uruguay judges may excuse an honorable person from punishment who has committed "a homicide

motivated by compassion, induced by repeated requests of the victim."

- In England and Wales anyone assisting a suicide risks up to fourteen years' imprisonment. However, suicide itself is not a crime, having been decriminalized in 1961.
- Assisted suicide is a crime in the Republic of Ireland.
- In Hungary assistance in suicide or attempted suicide is punishable by up to five years' imprisonment.
- The Northern Territory of Australia legalized voluntary euthanasia and assisted suicide for nine months until the Federal Parliament repealed the law in 1997.

Finding and Using Sources of Information

No matter what type of essay you are writing, it is necessary to find information to support your point of view. You can use sources such as books, magazine articles, newspaper articles, and online articles.

Using Books and Articles

You can find books and articles in a library by using the library's computer or cataloging system. If you are not sure how to use these resources, ask a librarian to help you. You can also use a computer to find many magazine articles and other articles written specifically for the Internet.

You are likely to find a lot more information you can possibly use in your essay, so your first task is to narrow your sources so you can spend your research time on what is likely to be the most usable material. Look at book and article titles. Look at book chapter titles, and examine the book's index to see if it contains information on the specific topic you want to write about. (For example, if you want to write about assisted suicide and you find a book about death and dying, check the chapter titles and index to be sure it contains information about assisted suicide before you bother to check out the book.)

For a five-paragraph essay, you don't need a great deal of supporting information, so quickly try to select a few good books and magazine or Internet articles. You don't need dozens. You might even find that one or two good books or articles contain all the information you need.

You probably don't have time to read an entire book, so find the chapters or sections that relate to your topic, and skim these. When you find useful information, copy it onto a note card or into a notebook. Look for supporting facts, statistics, quotations, and examples.

Using the Internet

When you select your supporting information, it is important that you evaluate its source. This is especially important with information you find on the Internet. Because nearly anyone can say nearly anything on the Internet, there is as much bad information as good information online. Before using Internet information—or any information—try to determine if the source is reliable. Is the author or Internet site sponsored by a legitimate organization? Is it a government source? Does the author have any special knowledge or training related to the topic you are looking up? Does the article indicate its own sources?

Using Your Supporting Information

When you use supporting information from a book, article, interview, or other source, there are three important things to remember:

1. *Make it clear whether you are using a direct quotation or a paraphrase.* If you copy information directly from your source, you are quoting it. You must put quotation marks around the information, and tell where the information comes from. If you put the information in your own words, you are paraphrasing it.

Here is an example of using a quotation:

One author who writes frequently about ethics believes that assisted suicide should be part of a society that grants its citizens the right to die when they choose: "Whether we are concerned to maximize liberty or to reduce suffering, we should prefer that the time when death comes depends on the wishes of mentally competent patients." (Singer)

Here is an example of a brief paraphrase of the same passage:

Author Peter Singer believes that assisted suicide should be part of a society that grants its citizens the right to choose when they die. He argues that as long as people are mentally competent to make such decisions, their right to control their own life should include the decision to end it. Only they truly know how much pain they are in, and only they should have the right to decide how the last months of their lives are spent.

2. *Use the information fairly*. Be careful to use supporting information in the way the author intended it. For example, it is unfair to quote an author as saying, "Assisted suicide should be legal" when he or she intended to say, "Assisted suicide should be legal *only in the rarest of cases.*" This is called taking information out of context. This is using supporting evidence unfairly.

3. *Give credit where credit is due*. Giving credit is known as citing. You must use citations when you use someone else's information, but not every piece of supporting information needs a citation.

    • If the supporting information is general knowledge—that is, it can be found in many sources— you do not have to cite your source.
    • If you directly quote a source, you must cite it.
    • If you paraphrase information from a specific source, you must cite it.

    If you do not use citations where you should, you are plagiarizing—or stealing—someone else's work.

Citing Your Sources

There are a number of ways to cite your sources. Your teacher will probably want you to do it in one of three ways:

• Informal: State in your own words where you got the information at the point where you use it in your essay.
• Informal list: At the end of the article, place an unnumbered list of the sources you used. This tells the reader where, in general, you got your information.

- Formal: Use an endnote. An endnote is generally placed at the end of an article or essay, although it may be located in different places depending on your teacher's requirements.

Works Cited

Singer, Peter. "Making Our Own Decisions About Death." *Free Inquiry* Aug.–Sept. 2005.

Using MLA Style to Create a Works Cited List

You will probably need to create a list of works cited for your paper. The entries in the list include materials that you quoted from, relied heavily on, or consulted to write your paper. There are several different ways to structure these references. The following examples are based on Modern Language Association (MLA) style, one of the major citation styles used by writers.

Book Entries

For most book entries you will need the author's name, the book's title, where it was published, what company published it, and the year it was published. This information is usually found on one of the first pages of the book. Variations on book entries include the following:

A book by a single author:
> Guest, Emma. *Children of AIDS: Africa's Orphan Crisis.* London: Sterling, 2003.

Two or more books by the same author:
> Friedman, Thomas L. *The World Is Flat: A Brief History of the Twentieth Century.* New York: Farrar, Straus and Giroux, 2005.
> ———, *From Beirut to Jerusalem.* New York: Doubleday, 1989.

A book by two or more authors:
> Pojman, Louis P., and Jeffrey Reiman. *The Death Penalty: For and Against.* Lanham, MD: Rowman & Littlefield, 1998.

A book with an editor:
> Friedman, Lauri S., ed. *At Issue: What Motivates Suicide Bombers?* San Diego: Greenhaven, 2004.

Periodical and Newspaper Entries

Entries for sources found in periodicals and newspapers are cited a bit differently than books. One difference is that these sources usually have both an article title and a publication name. They also may have specific dates and page ranges. Unlike book entries, these citations do not list where newspapers or periodicals are published or what company publishes them.

An article from a periodical:
>Snow, Keith Harmon. "State Terror in Ethiopia." *Z Magazine* June 2004: 33–35.

An unsigned article from a periodical:
>"Broadcast Decency Rules." *Issues & Controversies On File* 30 Apr. 2004.

An article from a newspaper:
>Constantino, Rebecca. "Fostering Love, Respecting Race." *Los Angeles Times* 14 Dec. 2002: B17.

Internet Sources

To document a source you found online, provide as much information on it as possible, including the author's name, the title of the document and/or the Web site, the date of publication or of last revision, the URL, and your date of access.

A Web source:
>Shyovitz, David. "The History and Development of Yiddish." Jewish Virtual Library 30 May 2005. < http://www.jewishvirtuallibrary.org/jsource/History/yiddish.html > .

Your teacher will tell you exactly how information should be cited in your essay. Generally, the very least information needed is the original author's name and the name of the article or other publication.

Be sure you know exactly what information your teacher requires before you start looking for your supporting information so that you know what information to copy alongside your notes.

Sample Essay Topics

Assisted Suicide Is Moral

Assisted Suicide Is Immoral

Assisted Suicide Promotes Dignity and Autonomy

Assisted Suicide Distorts the Meaning of Dignity and
Autonomy

Assisted Suicide Is Compassionate

Assisted Suicide Is Not Compassionate

Americans Should Have a Right to Die

Americans Should Have a Right to Life

Babies with Severe Birth Defects Should Be Eligible
for Assisted Suicide

Babies with Severe Birth Defects Should Not Be
Eligible for Assisted Suicide

States Should Be Allowed to Make Their Own Laws
About Assisted Suicide

States Should Not Be Allowed to Make Their Own
Laws About Assisted Suicide

Assisted Suicide Threatens the Disabled

Assisted Suicide Helps the Disabled

Legalized Assisted Suicide Would Lead to Abuses

Legalized Assisted Suicide Would Have Enough
Safeguards to Prevent Abuses

Assisted Suicide Would Discourage End-of-Life Care

Assisted Suicide Would Improve End-of-Life Care

Assisted Suicide Would Lead to Involuntary Killings

Assisted Suicide Would Save Health Costs

The Doctor-Patient Relationship Would Be
Jeopardized by Assisted Suicide

The Doctor-Patient Relationship Would Be
Strengthened by Assisted Suicide

Examining Assisted Suicide Around the World

Organizations to Contact

American Foundation for Suicide Prevention (AFSP)
120 Wall St., 22nd Fl., New York, NY 10005
(888) 333-AFSP • e-mail: inquiry@afsp.org
Web site: www.afsp.org

Formerly known as the American Suicide Foundation, AFSP opposes the legalization of physician-assisted suicide. AFSP publishes a policy statement on physician-assisted suicide, the newsletter *Crisis,* and the quarterly *Lifesavers.*

American Medical Association (AMA)
515 N. State St., Chicago, IL 60610 • (800) 621-8335
Web site: www.ama-assn.org

Founded in 1847, the AMA is the primary professional association of physicians in the United States. It opposes physician-assisted suicide.

Compassion & Choices
PO Box 101810, Denver, CO 80250-1810 • (800) 247-7421
Web site: www.compassionandchoices.org

Compassion & Choices believes that terminally ill adults who are mentally competent have the right to choose to die without pain and suffering. The organization does not promote or encourage suicide, but it does offer moral support to those who choose to intentionally hasten death.

Euthanasia Research and Guidance Organization (ERGO)
24829 Norris Ln., Junction City, OR 97448-9559
phone and fax: (541) 998-1873 • e-mail: ergo@efn.org
Web site: www.finalexit.org

ERGO advocates the passage of laws permitting physician-assisted suicide for the advanced terminally ill and the irreversibly ill who are suffering unbearably.

End-of-Life Choices
PO Box 101810, Denver, CO 80250-1810 • (800) 247-7421
email: info@endoflifechoices.org • Web site: www.end
oflifechoices.org/microsite/index.html

Advocates choices in dying for terminally ill, mentally competent persons. In addition to supporting appropriate pain and palliative care, the organization vocally promotes the right of these individuals to hasten their death under careful safeguards.

Human Life International (HLI)
4 Family Life Lane, Front Royal, VA 22630 • (800) 549-LIFE
e-mail: hli@hli.org • Web site: www.hli.org

The pro-life Human Life International is a research, educational, and service organization. It opposes euthanasia, infant euthanasia, and assisted suicide.

International Anti-Euthanasia Task Force (IAETF)
PO Box 760, Steubenville, OH 43952 • (740) 282-3810
e-mail: info@iaetf.org • Web site: www.iaetf.org

IAETF opposes the legalization of assisted suicide. It maintains an extensive and up-to-date library devoted solely to the issues surrounding euthanasia.

National Hospice Organization
1700 Diagonal Rd., Suite 625, Alexandria, VA 22314
(703) 837-1500 (phone) • e-mail: nhpco_info@nhpco.org
Web site: www.nho.org

The organization works to educate the public and health care professionals about the benefits of hospice care for the terminally ill and their families. It promotes the idea that, with proper care and pain medication, the terminally ill can live out their lives comfortably and in the company of their families.

National Right to Life
512 10th St. NW, Washington, DC 20004 • (202) 626-8800
e-mail: NRLC@nrlc.org • Web site: www.nrlc.org

National Right to Life opposes euthanasia, physician-assisted suicide, and abortion because it believes these practices disregard the value of human life.

The Right to Die Society of Canada

145 Macdonell Ave., Toronto, Ontario, Canada M6R 2A4
(416) 535-0690 • e-mail: contact-rtd@righttodie.ca
Web site: http://www.righttodie.ca/

The society supports the right of any mature individual who is chronically or terminally ill to choose the time, place, and means of his or her death.

Bibliography

Books

Battin, Margaret P., ed., *Death, Dying and the Ending of Life.* Hampshire, UK: Ashgate, 2006.

Cosic, Miriam, *The Right to Die: An Examination of the Euthanasia Debate.* London: New Holland, 2003.

Dowbiggin, Ian J., *A Concise History of Euthanasia: Life, Death, God, and Medicine.* Lanham, MD: Rowman & Littlefield, 2005.

Foley, Kathleen M., and Herbert Hendrin, eds., *The Case Against Assisted Suicide: For the Right to End-of-Life Care.* Baltimore: Johns Hopkins University Press, 2002.

Gailey, Elizabeth Atwood, *Write to Death: News Framing of the Right to Die Conflict, from Quinlan's Coma to Kevorkian's Conviction.* Westport, CT: Praeger, 2003.

Haley, James, ed., *Death and Dying: Opposing Viewpoints.* San Diego: Greenhaven, 2003.

Humphrey, Derek, *The Good Euthanasia Guide 2004: Where, What, and Who in Choices in Dying.* Junction City, OR: Norris Lane, 2004.

Olevitch, Barbara A., *Protecting Psychiatric Patients and Others from the Assisted-Suicide Movement: Insights and Strategies.* Westport, CT: Praeger, 2002.

Quill, Timothy E., and Margaret P. Battin, eds., *Physician-Assisted Dying: The Case for Palliative Care and Patient Choice.* Baltimore: Johns Hopkins University Press, 2004.

Rosenfeld, Barry, *Assisted Suicide and the Right to Die: The Interface of Social Science, Public Policy, and Medical Ethics.* Washington D.C.: American Psychological Association, 2004.

Somerville, Margaret, *Death Talk: The Case Against Euthanasia and Physician-Assisted Suicide.* Montreal: McGill-Queen's University Press, 2001.

Woodman, Sue, *Last Rights: The Struggle over the Right to Die.* New York: Perseus, 2001.

Woodward, John, ed., *At Issue: The Right to Die.* San Diego: Greenhaven, 2006.

Periodicals

Carosa, Alberto, "Letter from the Netherlands: From Mercy Killing to Euthanasia," *Chronicles,* March 2005.

Coren, Michael, "Never Say Die, or Right to Die," *Toronto Sun,* December 18, 2004.

Ferry, Carol Bernstein, "A Good Death," *Nation,* September 17, 2001.

Gross, Judy, "Life or Death? Twice She Had to Make Critical Decision," *National Catholic Reporter,* April 1, 2005.

Holt, Jim, "Euthanasia for Babies?" *New York Times Magazine,* July 10, 2005.

Johnson, Boris, "Assisted Suicide Is Problematic, But Better than Months of Agony," *Daily Telegraph (London),* January 26, 2006.

Keizer, Garret, "Life Everlasting: The Religious Right and the Right to Die," *Harper's,* February 2005.

Menzel, Paul T., "Determining the Value of Life," *Free Inquiry,* August/September 2005.

Ponnuru, Romesh, "Reasons to Live," *National Review,* April 25, 2005.

Radtke, Richard, "A Case Against Physician-Assisted Suicide," *Journal of Disability Policy Studies,* Summer 2005.

Rollin, Betty, "Path to a Peaceful Death," *Washington Post,* May 30, 2004.

Saunders, Debra, "Death Trumps Choice," *San Francisco Chronicle,* January 6, 2005.

Singer, Peter, "Law Reform, or DIY Suicide," *Free Inquiry,* February/March 2005.

Smith, Wesley J., "The Oregon Tall Tale: The Creepy Underside of Legal Assisted Suicide," *Weekly Standard,* May 17, 2004.

Smoker, Barbara, "On Advocating Infant Euthanasia," *Free Inquiry*, December 2003/January 2004.

Springer, Thomas, "Killing with Kindness," *Christianity Today*, December 2004.

Wilson, Libby, and Jim McBeth, "Do I Believe in the Concept of Assisted Euthanasia?" *Mail on Sunday (London)*, January 29, 2006.

Web Sites

Assisted Suicide (www.assistedsuicide.org). A Web page maintained by the Euthanasia Research & Guidance Organization (ERGO), this pro–assisted suicide site contains articles on euthanasia and assisted suicide in the United States and around the world.

Californians Against Assisted Suicide (www.ca-aas.com). A coalition of groups that oppose the legalization of assisted suicide in California.

Dying with Dignity (www.dyingwithdignity.ca). Dying with Dignity seeks public support to legally permit voluntary physician-assisted dying in Canada. The site offers many articles, fact sheets, and reports on the topic, along with links to other pro–assisted suicide organizations.

State of Oregon: Physician Assisted Suicide (www.oregon.gov/DHS/ph/pas/). The official site for Oregon's Death with Dignity Act. Under the act, which was passed in 1997, terminally ill Oregon residents are allowed to obtain prescriptions for self-administered, lethal medications from their physicians. The Web site contains information, statistics, and other state reports about the act.

Index

Smith, Wesley J., 24
Sowers, Wesley, 54, 68
Stevens, Kenneth, 51
suicide
  assisted dying vs., 55
  depression as leading cause of, 51

see also physician-assisted suicide
Switzerland, physician-assisted suicide in, provisions of, 21

T
Taira, Gayle, 39

Picture Credits

About the Editor

Lauri S. Friedman earned her bachelor's degree in religion and political science from Vassar College. Much of her studies there focused on political Islam, and she produced a thesis on the Islamic Revolution in Iran titled *Neither West, Nor East, But Islam*. She also holds a preparatory degree in flute performance from the Manhattan School of Music, and is pursuing a master's degree in history at San Diego State University. She has edited over ten books for Greenhaven Press, including *At Issue: What Motivates Suicide Bombers?*, *At Issue: How Should the United States Treat Prisoners in the War on Terror?*, and *Introducing Issues with Opposing Viewpoints: Terrorism*. She currently lives near the beach in San Diego with her boyfriend, Randy, and their yellow lab, Trucker.